The
Poker
Diaries

THE

Poker

DIARIES

♦ ♠ ♥ ♣

Liza Conrad

nal
jam
books

NAL Jam

Published by New American Library, a division of Penguin Group (USA) Inc., 375 Hudson Street, New York, New York 10014, USA • Penguin Group (Canada), 90 Eglinton Avenue East, Suite 700, Toronto, Ontario M4P 2Y3, Canada (a division of Pearson Penguin Canada Inc.) • Penguin Books Ltd., 80 Strand, London WC2R 0RL, England • Penguin Ireland, 25 St. Stephen's Green, Dublin 2, Ireland (a division of Penguin Books Ltd.) • Penguin Group (Australia), 250 Camberwell Road, Camberwell, Victoria 3124, Australia (a division of Pearson Australia Group Pty. Ltd.). Penguin Books India Pvt. Ltd., 11 Community Centre, Panchsheel Park, New Delhi - 110 017, India • Penguin Group (NZ), cnr Airborne and Rosedale Roads, Albany, Auckland 1310, New Zealand (a division of Pearson New Zealand Ltd.) • Penguin Books (South Africa) (Pty.) Ltd., 24 Sturdee Avenue, Rosebank, Johannesburg 2196, South Africa • Penguin Books Ltd., Registered Offices: 80 Strand, London WC2R 0RL, England

First published by NAL Jam, an imprint of New American Library,
a division of Penguin Group (USA) Inc.

First Printing, January 2007
1 3 5 7 9 10 8 6 4 2

NAL JAM and logo are trademarks of Penguin Group (USA) Inc.

LIBRARY OF CONGRESS CATALOGING-IN-PUBLICATION DATA:
Conrad, Liza.
The poker diaries / Liza Conrad.
p. cm.
ISBN-13: 978-0-451-22024-0 (trade pbk.)
[1. Poker—Fiction. 2. Gambling—Fiction. 3. Social classes—Fiction 4. Dating (Social customs)—Fiction.
5. Family life—New York (N.Y.)—Fiction. 6. New York (N.Y.)—Fiction.] I. Title.
PZ7.C764744Pok 2007
[Fic]—dc22   2006014574

Set in Bembo
Designed by Spring Hoteling
Printed in the United States of America

Dedicated to all my nieces and nephews:
Tyler, Zachary, Tori, Cassidy, Pannos, Eva, and Sofia.
And, as always, to Alexa, Nicholas, Isabella, and Jack

Acknowledgments

I'd like to thank Anne Bohner, my editor at NAL, who pushed me to make this book the best it could be, and whose insights are always so valuable.

Of course, the wonderful Jay Poynor, my agent—he's been my friend and supporter since my very first novel.

I must thank my family—my huge extended family—because I can't recall a Thanksgiving that didn't end with a large and loud game of poker. Turkey and poker. Only in my family.

My usual suspects of friends: From Writers' Cramp, Pammie, Gina, Jon; Kathy J.; Kathy L.; Kerri; Cleo; Nanc . . . everyone. You all know who you are.

And finally, to my beloved J.D. We've been together so long I kind of forget any memories without you in them. You have the kindest soul, and when I'm with you, I'm at peace. And you make a really good martini.

Poker Hands

(from lowest to highest)

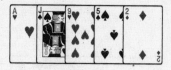

HIGH CARD

ONE PAIR

TWO PAIR

THREE OF A KIND

STRAIGHT

Flush

Full House

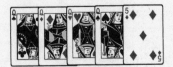

Four of a Kind

Straight Flush

Royal Flush

Prologue

You know that ad campaign, "What happens in Vegas stays in Vegas"? I'm living proof that's not quite true.

My parents met on a New York–to–Los Angeles flight fifteen years and nine months or so ago. My mother, a museum curator, was going to view the private art collection of some rich dead guy. My father was going to play in an illegal poker tournament, though he didn't tell her that. He also didn't tell her about the outstanding warrant for his arrest in New Jersey, or that his nickname was Blackjack.

They were flying first-class and, at least how Dad tells the story, they were drinking a *lot* of free champagne. By the time they landed, they got the bright idea to tell my father's waiting limo driver to take them to elope in Las Vegas. Needless to say, *more* champagne was waiting in the back of the limo. By the time they realized this was all a very, very bad idea, my mother had the flu. Then she told herself it was an ulcer from too much stress at her job. And then, when she couldn't lie to herself anymore, she took a pregnancy test. I am a souvenir from the one, lone impetuous act my mother has ever done in her life. A souvenir of Vegas. And I didn't stay in Vegas. Nope, I came along nine months later back in New York. So much for that slogan.

I give my parents credit: They tried to work it out for a year. My father dressed up in tuxedos and went to museum exhibit openings, even though his idea of art is that painting of the dogs playing poker.

My mother, for her part, tried to learn that a flush beats a straight. She let my father's buddies come to our Central Park West apartment for poker night once a week—even though she cringed at the cigar smoke and foul language. But even that was a disaster, because the first time my dad asked her to make some snacks for his poker night (he was thinking peanuts and chips and maybe a six-foot-long sub with extra salami), she served caviar with toast points and endive lettuce with lobster salad.

When I was a couple of months old, my parents got divorced, but in all these years they've never, ever said a bad word about the other one. I live with my mom on the Upper West Side of Manhattan during the week, and every other weekend, and for a month each summer, I go off with my dad to his neighborhood in Clinton—what used to be called Hell's Kitchen—and sometimes to Atlantic City or Las Vegas.

I love both my parents. When I was little, my mom never let me read the back of the cereal box during breakfast. Instead, she'd open up a big, glossy coffee-table art book that weighed more than I did, I think, to a page on Degas, or Michelangelo, or some other artist, and she would teach me. She'd say, "Lulu, look how the Flemish painters' portraits look almost like photographs." Or she'd tell me about Goya, her favorite painter of all, and of his "mad" period when he supposedly painted himself out of insanity. She brought me to museums and galleries, and we took trips to places like Venice and Florence.

When I would visit my dad, he'd teach me how to shuffle cards, or how to pick a horse at the race-track in Belmont. He taught me how to fill out the box scores at Yankees games, while we ate hot dogs and Cracker Jack. He'd take me to jazz clubs and to boxing gyms. I was even with him when he got my name tattooed on his right bicep, right below my mom's name.

But as cool as all this might sound, and as lucky as I am that my parents are divorced but still really like each other, I knew that one day my downtown world with Dad would come colliding into my uptown world with Mom. Which was why I tried to tell her that dating New York City's most eligible bachelor was a very bad idea. Almost as bad as eloping with my father to Las Vegas. But my mother didn't listen, which was why I was now *this close* to calling the mayor of New York my new stepdad. And why my life got completely and totally out of control.

I'm Lulu King, and my life is the Poker Diaries.

Chapter One

Lulu's Rule of Poker #1:
When playing strip poker, wear a sexy bra.

"I fold." My best downtown friend, Angie, tossed her cards at me.

I looked over at Dack, my best uptown buddy. He shook his head. "I'm in, but I think I'm in trouble. Go on, Lulu. I call."

I laid down my cards. "Full boat. Pretty ladies over eights."

"Oh damn!" Dack snapped. He pulled off his T-shirt.

"Call it a night?" I asked playfully.

"No!" he groused. "I can still make a comeback."

"For the record, Dack," I said, smiling my best obnoxious grin, "you are wearing a pair of plaid flannel boxers. And socks. And nothing else. Angie over here is in a bra, yes, but she's also in jeans, socks, sneakers, and a scarf." Angie was no dummy. She knew if she took off her shirt first, Dack would be paying more attention to her red lace Victoria's Secret bra than his cards.

"And I am fully clothed. As in, I think I've lost my gloves. And that's it."

"And *every* time we play strip poker, we end up like this," Angie said. "The only reason you don't wind up stark naked is that Lulu here always feels sorry for you when you get down to your boxers and offers to call it a night."

"All right," Dack snapped at us. "Let's put in the movie and order takeout."

Dack—an acronym for Dalton Angus Charles Kensington III—started getting dressed. Angie pulled on her NYU sweatshirt.

"I was hoping you'd stay in your bra for the heck of it, Angie," he said to her, winking and smirking.

"Dream on, Ralph," she answered back. She likes to annoy him by calling him Ralph—as in Lauren;

he wears it a lot. Angie is a total thrift-store junkie—
the complete opposite. Dack is a blond with a neat
haircut and clear skin and green eyes. He looks like
he could model for Ralph. Angie would be better
in an ad for United Colors of Benetton. She usually
has at least two colors going on in her hair, and right
now she was sporting cornrows with tribal beads.
She also had a belly-button piercing, a tiny diamond
stud in her nose, and a tattoo that she refused to show
Dack unless he *earned* a peek by beating her at strip
poker. I was with her when she got it. It's a Chinese
symbol for *warrior* right on her rear end.

The three of us went into the den of Dack's
apartment. Calling it an apartment is sort of like saying the pope is a priest with a fancier hat. Dack's
apartment is two whole floors of the Kensington
Towers. When you walk in, it's wall-to-wall antiques.
Some decorator made the cover of *Manhattan Living*
with it. Dack's dad was the founder and president of
a company that invented an Internet search engine,
as well as computer software and spyware. When he
sold his company, he got a sum with a *B* in front
of it—billion. Then his dad retired, traded in Dack's
mom for the requisite trophy wife (we call her Baywatch, as the only thing she seems to be good for is

looking hot in her bathing suit), and spends most of his time on the golf course or his yacht. Dack's mom, in her own words, "took the big jerk to the cleaners." Hence Dack's colossal apartment and the cover of a magazine.

"You going to your dad's this weekend?" Dack asked as we flopped onto the enormous leather couch in the den, and he turned on the equally enormous plasma-screen television to MTV.

I nodded.

"Which means she's gonna see Mark," Angie said.

Mark is my downtown crush. He just turned seventeen, and he's got a record—albeit not a very serious one. He once spray-painted a wall with the New York Yankees logo during the World Series. Dumb, but forgivable, given what a fanatic he is for the Yanks. He's barely passing high school with mostly Ds, and he does some work for my dad. He collects cards during football season. He goes around to all the bars in Hell's Kitchen that take illegal football bets, and he collects the money and the cards—the forms where people write down their picks. Besides that, Mark plays poker. And he's good. Almost as good as I am. I see him during some of the backroom tournaments and games my dad plays in—and sometimes I play, too.

"When are you going to take me to your dad's poker club?" Dack asked.

"When you learn how to bluff," I shot back at him.

"I know how to bluff."

"Please." Angie snorted. "I'm lousy at poker, but even *I* can tell when you have a bad hand. You always raise like crazy, hoping everyone else will get scared and fold."

"You guys are wrong. I played last week with Tyler and Grant, and I cleaned them out. I won two hundred dollars playing Hold 'Em."

Angie sighed. "You don't get it, do you, Ralph? They're seconds and thirds."

"What are you talking about, Angie?" he asked her.

"Seconds and thirds," I explained. "What Angie calls all you trust-funders. You know, Tyler David Smith the Second and Grant Wellington Fairchild the Third."

"So?" Dack said. "What does that have to do with anything?"

Angie rolled her eyes. "You think Tyler and Grant

are hard-core poker players like Lulu and Mark and her dad? They're chumps . . . and so are you, boxer-shorts boy."

Dack's face turned red. Sometimes Angie can be harsh. But once you get to know her, she's really fun.

"I'll show you who can play in the big league," Dack said.

"Come on, let's just watch the movie. Please? Angie, drop it. Dack . . . don't get all freaked out. Chill . . . both of you." Dack definitely took things too seriously sometimes. Most especially losing.

Dack stood and popped in a DVD of *the Texas Chainsaw Massacre* remake. We ordered Chinese delivery. We ate popcorn and drank a ton of caffeine and Red Bull. I thought it was all forgotten.

But Dack hadn't forgotten at all. And I had no idea just what a mess he was about to get us all into.

Chapter Two

Lulu's Rule of Poker #2:
Don't bet what you can't afford to lose.

"**D**o you like David, darling?" My mom was putting in her diamond drop earrings, sitting at her dressing table in her bedroom. I was flopped on her bed eating crunchy peanut butter out of the jar with a spoon—which drives her nuts.

"David? As in Mr. Big Apple, the mayor, the king of Manhattan? The one who Dad says is taking his promise to get tough on crime just a little too seriously? That David?"

"Yes, that David," she snapped. "And stop eating peanut butter out of the jar."

"Dad lets me."

"Yes. And Dad also lets you stay up until three a.m. and feeds you Nathan's hot dogs for breakfast."

"That's not true. By the time we wake up, it's more like brunch."

"Tallulah Elizabeth King, you know very well which David I mean, and you know very well that as much as I adore your father he is hardly the poster boy for the food pyramid."

"Do you know you only call me Tallulah when I'm bugging you?"

She sighed and looked at herself in the mirror, pulling back on the skin by her eyes.

"Don't," I said.

"Don't what?"

"Don't even think about getting a face-lift or Botox or any of that junk or you'll end up like Dack's mom. Her face looks like she ironed it."

My mother is a cool blonde, sort of like the old movie actress Grace Kelly, or the French actress Catherine Deneuve. She has her hair highlighted to perfection every few weeks at a salon so snooty you have to have a referral in order to be accepted as a client there. My whole life, I don't ever recall seeing her with a hair out of place, or without makeup. I don't think she's ever even chipped a nail. She was educated at the Sorbonne and speaks perfect French, as well as Italian. She's the type of woman who walks into a room and everyone turns around.

Me? I have Dad's completely unruly curls—black. He deals with his hair by shaving it all off. Very tough-guy cool. He kind of looks like an action movie star. I deal with my untamable hair by wearing it in a ponytail most of the time. I have Mom's hazel eyes. But I am most definitely more downtown than uptown. I shop in Greenwich Village for vintage. And I occasionally raid Dad's closet for his old leather jackets and any other interesting stuff. Of course, at the school my mother makes me go to, I have to wear a uniform, which I hate.

My mother reapplied her ruby Chanel lipstick. "I would never want to end up like one of those face-lift junkies, but I wouldn't mind getting rid of a few crow's-feet."

"Mom, the mayor is crazy about you. He could have any woman in Manhattan, and he picked you."

"I know. But they're like vultures around him, really, darling. Vultures. Does he have to look like

Hugh Grant? Give him an English accent and there'd be no hope for this romance whatsoever. Some twenty-something would steal him away."

"Like Mr. Kensington and Baywatch?"

"Bay-who?"

"Baywatch, his new wife."

"Lulu! Is that what you kids call her?"

I nodded, laughing. "Fits, don't you think?"

Mom was friendly with Dack's mom. Despite herself, I saw her eyes twinkling. "Well, it's not very nice, but ... yes. Mr. Kensington certainly did his thinking with his ... well, you know."

"Yeah, but the mayor's different, Mom. What does Page Six say?" I was talking about the bible of New York gossip. "The mayor likes brains with his beauty."

"Thanks, Lulu. So you do like him."

I shrugged. "A little too perfect for me. But if you're happy ..."

"Well, I am, Lulu. It's just that for the first time since your father, he's someone I could get serious with."

"Great." Of course, it was anything *but* great. "Mom, can I ask you something?"

"Anything, Lulu. You know that."

"I mean, my whole life, I've known that you were the one great love of Dad's life. He has your name tattooed on his arm, for God's sake. And I've never even seen you interested in anyone else until now. I'm mature enough to know you and Dad could never, ever live together or get back together. But . . . well . . . the mayor is so *different* from Dad. It's like he's the polar opposite. So I guess I wonder how it is you could love him if he's nothing like the love of your life."

My mom turned around on her chair to face me. "Oh, Lulu . . . you know, your father will always be the one crazy passion of my life. I would see him across a crowded room and completely lose my train of thought. But we were so different. Relationships take work, and you have to spend time together. I mean, that's why you get married. You have someone to share life with. Only your father really wanted nothing to do with my life and the things that interest me, like Broadway, museums, art, travel—and I don't mean to Atlantic City. And I could care less whether the poker hand where they're all the same— you know, diamond or heart—beats the one where they're in order."

I rolled my eyes. "Flush, Mom. The one where

they're all the same suit is a flush. The one where they're in order is a straight. And the one where they're all in order *and* the same suit is a straight flush. And that's a very good hand."

"Exactly. I can't make myself be interested in that and playing pool and the racetrack and smelly cigars. We're just from two different worlds. But David . . . he's handsome and smart. And no, I don't necessarily feel the world stop spinning when I see him across a crowded room, but I love being with him, and we can talk for hours and hours and never run out of things to say. And he's a good man, Lulu. He really is."

"I'm happy for you, Mom."

"But do you like him?"

I shrugged. "I guess so. I don't know him really well yet, Mom. The only times I see him are when we go to charity events and stuff. And there are usually a bunch of people around."

"Precisely. Which is why he suggested arranging some time alone together, just the two of you. I knew you'd agree."

Trapped! I cringed inside. I couldn't imagine doing anything with the mayor of New York. I mean, what? Teach him how to play poker?

"Well, off I go." She stood. She was wearing a black velvet Valentino gown with a diamond necklace that belonged to my great-grandmother.

"What's tonight again?"

"Cocktail party at Gracie Mansion to celebrate the United Nations anniversary."

"Have a good time."

"I will, Lulu." My mother bent over and pecked the top of my head. "Your father is picking you up?"

I nodded.

"No OTB parlors."

"Sure, Mom."

"See you Sunday. And don't forget you have the paper due Monday in English."

"I won't."

As soon as she left, I went to my room to grab my backpack. The rest of Mom's and my apartment is decorated in French country. I'm not sure what that is exactly, but the furniture is a lot of pale wood, and the walls are pretty blues and florals. And I am quite sure my mother's interior decorator used to have to pop a tranquilizer to deal with my room every time he walked past it.

My bedroom is what my mother terms "early slob." Every Tuesday and Thursday our housekeeper

17

comes, but Mom tells her to just forget my room because it's beyond help. Mom doesn't understand that I know exactly where everything is, and there's an order to my chaos. She just thinks it's a nuclear explosion. My shelves are lined with the stuff I get when I'm with Dad—souvenir shot glasses from Atlantic City, next to cheesy plastic snow globes and a set of glasses that, when you add ice, the men lose their clothes. Dad made me promise never to add ice in the vicinity of Mom. On the walls, though, are my art posters. I have one of the sunflower prints by van Gogh, and a Dalí poster—the guy who paints clocks melting all over the place.

I threw my favorite T-shirt in my backpack, along with my iPod, and put on my leather boots. The doorman called up about twenty minutes later to tell me Dad was there. I picked up my stuff and left my apartment, locking up behind me and taking the elevator down to the lobby. As if my parents weren't already completely different, their families added into the mix were even more complicated. Mom and I live in a building of marble floors and hushed whispers. She inherited it from her father—he's still alive, but this was one of his real estate holdings. My mother's family is as old as New York itself. Supposedly, my great-great-grandfather once owned most of Wall Street.

Dad's family, on the other hand ... Well, my grandfather served time in Sing Sing Correctional. Apparently he shot a man in self-defense, only no one believed it was self-defense on account of the bullet entering the other guy in the *back* as he was running away. Grandpa now owns a bar. I think there's a law about convicted felons not being able to get a liquor license, so I'm not sure who he bribed or how it happened, but King's Pub, with its green neon shamrock in the window, is like my second home. My grandmother on that side died a few years ago, and my grandfather is now as bad as my dad when it comes to spoiling me—not that I mind.

The elevator opened with a near-silent whoosh. I walked through the lobby and gave my dad a hug.

"Hey, Lulu." He kissed me. "Come on; we got a big night ahead of us." He wrapped an arm around my shoulders, and I waved good-bye to Jacques, the doorman.

Waiting outside was my father's motorcycle, a black Harley with a lot of chrome. I put on my helmet while Dad started the bike, and then I climbed on in back of him.

I may have been conceived in Las Vegas, but New York is in my blood. It's how I breathe. I love the museums and the world of my mother, but more than that, I love the world of my father. I like to watch the people walking along, all different colors, fashions, and sizes. I love passing a drag queen in the Village, her makeup done to perfection, her eyebrows as perfect as a movie star's, her false lashes batting at me as we zoom past.

I like seeing the speed chess players in Washington Square Park near NYU. In the summer, when Dad takes me through Central Park, I like watching the Frisbee players and the New Yorkers walking barefoot in the grass, an oasis of green in our concrete jungle. There's a contagious joy as everyone sheds their winter coats for the warmth and lushness of a new season.

At night I look into the windows of apartments as we ride past. In the dark I can see the lit rooms and the faces of people in their kitchens, or mothers walking crying babies across the floor, or artists at work painting canvases. It's a bit like being a voyeur, as if the city were composed of shadow boxes and moving dolls inside.

I hugged my dad as we drove toward his neighborhood. The wind whipped against my face, and I could smell the city's restaurants—Thai, Italian, Chinese, and French. Men and women dined at tables on the sidewalk, and I saw people walking tiny little mops of dogs, some in comical little sweaters, and even a guy with a Great Dane.

Finally we arrived on the West Side, the area Dad calls home. He drove to King's Pub and parked.

Walking inside, I could hear the jukebox blaring Frank Sinatra. A quirky thing about King's: You can hear only Sinatra or Bruce Springsteen. That's it. You see, my grandfather loaded the jukebox with all Sinatra music. Then, when I was old enough to complain about nothing cool being on the jukebox, my grandfather said to me, "Lulu, you can have A-one to A-eight. Eight songs. One artist. Pick."

So I loaded it with, at the time, Green Day. Then I was in my Eminem phase—Grandpa really hated that. I moved on to a brief Good Charlotte period. Right now it's Springsteen.

My grandfather was standing behind the bar.

"Lulu!" He beamed. I ran over to him and stepped up on the bar rail and kissed him on the cheek. He has the word DEATH tattooed across his knuckles on one hand, but he has LIFE tattooed on the other hand, and LULU beneath a heart on his forearm.

He poured me a Coke without my having to ask and then nodded toward the back of the bar.

"Got a great game going on."

"Oh?" I raised my eyebrow.

"You in?"

"What do you think?" My grandfather and father taught me everything I know about poker, and Grandpa and I have a deal: He bankrolls me . . . and we split the profits. He envisions me one day being the first King family member in the World Series of Poker. Legit. As in, not an illegal backroom game. I kind of like the idea, though I'd never tell Mom that. She envisions me going to the Sorbonne and being the first King to be a Rhodes scholar.

I looked down the bar. Dad was talking to a few buddies of his, so I wandered into the back room. It's completely illegal to have a high-stakes poker game going on, but Grandpa never was too concerned about the law. A cop or two has even been known to play. Three tables had action at once. I stood and surveyed the gamblers. A couple of them, regulars, either winked at me or gave me a nod.

Sitting at one table was Mark. I waited until he

noticed me. He was looking down at his cards intensely. He has jet-black hair that he wears a little long, and a silver earring in his left ear. He has a tribal tattoo encircling his right arm, and usually wears plain black T-shirts and Levi's. Dark brown eyes and a dimple on his left cheek complete the package. Hot with a capital H.

He decided to fold and then looked up. "I'm sittin' this one out," he said, then rose and walked over to me.

"Hey, Lulu."

"Hi."

"You playin' tonight?"

"Sure. You losin'?" I teased.

"Nah. I'm taking your money. Of course"—he leaned over and whispered in my ear—"I'd be happy to take it out in trade—a simple kiss for all the chips."

I leaned back and winked. "We'll have to see if you're in any position to bargain."

He laughed and went back and sat down. I would likely end up at his table with Slick Finnegan, an old friend of my father's. He was an okay player who hid behind mirrored shades. Then there was Louie Smalls, who wasn't small at all; nor was that his last name. He weighed at least four hundred pounds. Everyone has a nickname at the table. They call Mark "the Kid" because he's young to be playing against the old-timers like my dad and Louie. Mark was raised on the game, though. His dad, who left for Las Vegas a long time ago and hasn't been back since, taught him how to play. Mark's mother lives with her new boyfriend. So Mark lives with his grandma, who's a sweet lady, but at eighty-one, she's just a little too old to keep Mark out of trouble—and away from poker games.

I listened to the sound of chips hitting one another, and smelled cigar smoke wafting through the air. I loved it, everything about it.

Suddenly my cell phone vibrated against my hip. I picked it up, and caller ID said it was Dack. I stepped out of the back room and into the bar.

"Hello?"

"Lulu?"

"Hold on, Dack. I can barely hear you." I maneuvered my way through the bar and out onto the sidewalk.

"What's up?" I asked. Usually when I was at my dad's, I didn't talk to Dack as often.

"Lulu." I heard the panic in his voice. "Man . . . I'm in a lot of trouble."

"What?" I envisioned him forgetting a term paper, but at the same time, his voice was so upset.

"Listen . . . I played in a poker game tonight."

"Uh-huh."

"Remember how you always say, 'Never bet what you can't afford to lose'?"

"Yeah."

"Well, I didn't listen. I lost something tonight. Big-time. Lulu, I'm in a whole mess of trouble."

Chapter Three

Lulu's Rule of Poker #3:
At the table, you don't have friends—just opponents.

"What are you talking about?" I asked.

"One of the guys from school runs with this crowd. A little tougher, a little older. You know J.T.?"

"Yeah."

"Well, his older brother, Carter, has been to rehab a few times, been in jail. He hangs with some guys. They heard I played poker, so they invited me to sit in on a high-stakes game."

I groaned. "I don't like where this story is going, Dack."

"Yeah, well, I hate where this story is going, 'cause I know the ending. You know how I keep thinking I'm ready for the big time? I'm not."

"I could have told you that and saved you some grief, Dack. What am I saying? I *have* told you that."

"I know. I should have listened."

"How much did you lose?"

"It's not how much. It's *what*."

"I have a feeling this is about more than a pair of boxer shorts. Please just tell me, Dack."

"Okay. I lost six hundred dollars."

"Ouch."

"Yeah. It was stupid of me to bring that much—if my mom finds out I took that much out of my savings account, she'll kill me. Then they started saying things like, 'Go home, rich boy.' So I got mad. And I bet my grandfather's watch."

"Oh, Dack, you didn't."

"I did. And of course, I lost. Lulu . . . I can't tell my grandfather I lost that watch, let alone lost it gambling. I'll be disowned."

"I doubt that. He'll be mad, but he'd get over it."

"No. He'll hate me forever. And if he ever did get over it, I can promise you my mother won't. It'll send her to her shrink three times a week instead of just two."

Dack's grandfather's watch was one of Dack's prized possessions. It wasn't just that it was a beautiful Rolex. On the back of it was inscribed a note from President John F. Kennedy. Dack's grandfather had been an ambassador during JFK's administration. It wasn't just a watch; it was a piece of history.

"Maybe we can buy the watch back from them. Just pray they haven't read the inscription."

"I don't think they would let me buy it back. They probably wouldn't sell it to me just to make a point about rich boys gambling. I just have to get that watch back, Lulu."

"All right. Let me think on it. I'll figure something out."

"Okay. You coming home tomorrow?"

"Sunday morning. How about if I come over around two?"

"Okay. See you then."

"See ya. Try not to worry."

I shut my phone. I felt bad for Dack. Since his father married Baywatch, Dack rarely saw him. The way Dack figured it, Baywatch was going to pump out a baby, and then his father would be lost to him forever. I told him to try not to worry. I couldn't imagine Baywatch sacrificing her perfect figure for a baby, let alone giving up her caffeine addiction and cigarettes during pregnancy. Not only that, I don't think you're allowed to dye your hair when you're pregnant. No way would she let her dark roots show.

I went back into the bar. The place was packed. My grandfather was behind the bar telling his infamous time-he-met-Sinatra story. I waited until he finished; then I said, "Grandpa, I want to go sit in."

"Sure thing, Lulu. I consider giving you my hard-earned money a surer thing than the bank. I almost always get a very nice return on my investment." He said it loudly—it's his way of bragging about me to all his crazy buddies in the bar.

He went to the register and counted out ten twenty-dollar bills, and also handed me a stack of fives.

"Go get 'em, Lulu."

I grinned, took the money, and headed toward the back room. My father sat at one table with a pile of chips in front of him. Dad is a good poker player, but even he says I'm better. I didn't know why for a long time, and then, oddly enough, I found out why at Career Day at school. And no, there wasn't a professional poker player there.

FBI Special Agent in Charge Lucas Antonelli came to school along with a lot of other different professionals. Given that it was the exclusive, hopelessly snobby Baxter Academy, there were a few investment bankers, computer moguls (Dack's dad even came in), representatives of assorted other careers where you make a lot of bucks and wear a suit. But I decided to go to the FBI session, figuring it would be interesting.

Agent Antonelli gave us a personality quiz, and then he showed us an interactive video in which we had to decide whether the person being interrogated was telling the truth or lying. Anyway, between my score on the video and the personality quiz, he said I'd make an excellent FBI profiler. When I asked him why, he said I innately read people better than most trained professionals. More than that, even, he said I went with my gut and didn't second-guess myself.

That helps me at the poker table. I can read my opponents really well; I'm quick at math and figuring out odds; and on top of that, I've learned from playing poker since kindergarten that my gut instinct is usually right. It's why I did well on my PSATs. If I take a multiple-choice exam, I know to go with my gut.

I looked over at Mark's table. He winked at me and made a slight head movement to his left. I could see that the guy next to him was close to losing it all. He had almost no chips left, and he looked pretty drunk—which is a fatal mistake a lot of gamblers who *lose* make. Why do you think you can drink for *free* at the tables in Atlantic City and Vegas? The drunker you are, the less likely you are to trust your gut and good sense, and the more likely you are to bet big and bet stupid.

I waited patiently. Sure enough, the drunk guy lost, and then he said, "That's it for me, boys. I'm headin' home." He got up and half staggered to the door. I immediately sat down in his vacant chair and said, "Deal me in."

Another rule of poker is, no matter *how* cute your opponent might be, no matter that he looks sinfully delicious with that adorable dimple of his, in the end, it's his hand of cards versus yours. So though I was flirting with Mark all night, I kept my head on the game.

We played for three hours straight, and I was up by about four hundred dollars. Technically I had to give my grandfather half. So I was up two hundred dollars. Mark was winning, too, and we effectively chased two other players from the table because they were losing big-time.

After they left, Mark asked me, "Want to go get something to eat?"

Out of the corner of my eye, I saw Dad rise from his table. "Can't. I'm sure my dad is ready to call it a night. What time is it?"

"It's only midnight."

"I'd love to, but I should get going."

"Will I see you tomorrow night?"

"Probably. My dad wants to come here to watch the fights on cable."

"Great. I'll see you then. Maybe we can play a few hands. If I win, I told you . . . one kiss."

"And if I win?" I teased, my heart beating hard.

"You'll have to decide what you want, Lulu."

I couldn't think of anything to say, so I looked at his tattoo. "You'd have to tattoo my name on your arm." I grinned at him.

"I think that could be arranged." He grinned back.

I wondered if he had any secret tattoos elsewhere, but before I could ask, my dad came over to us.

"Time to go, Lulu."

"Sure, Dad . . . Night, Mark."

"Good night, Lulu. Good game."

"Thanks."

My father wrapped an arm around my shoulders, and we said good-bye to my grandfather. We went out to Dad's bike and rode it the fifteen blocks to his place.

Whereas Mom's apartment is full of art and antiques, silk and chandeliers, Dad's place is . . . well, he calls it "early bachelor." He's got a leather couch and armchair perfectly worn in where he either lies or sits watching sports on television. On the walls are mostly photos of me. It's highly embarrassing. There's the typical first-grade, missing-my-two-front-teeth class picture. And one from my chubby phase. And a picture of me in my Halloween costume the year I went as a pumpkin.

"Hungry?" Dad asked, opening the fridge. "I could whip up some hot dogs and macaroni and cheese. Or maybe a salami sandwich on rye. Have some good, hot deli mustard."

"Nah. I'm okay." My mother marveled how neither Dad nor I had an ulcer from the food we ate.

"You know, Lulu . . . I love ya."

"Love you, too, Dad."

"Good. Then you won't mind me saying I don't want you getting involved with Mark."

"What? What are you talking about?"

"Look . . . I see how you two are together. Big-time sparks. Like your mom and me. And that's trouble, especially at your age. Plus, he's not good enough for you. He's a punk. He's from the neighborhood."

"Excuse me?" I couldn't believe what I was hearing. "Let me get this straight . . . I live part of my life here in this neighborhood, but you don't really want me having anything to do with the people here?"

"I'm not saying that. I'm just saying stick to boys from that school of yours. The future Trumps."

"Why? So I can one day end up with a man with a bad comb-over?"

"No. So you end up with someone going places. And by places, I don't mean the state pen."

"Dad, Mark's a nice guy. He looks up to you."

"I know. I like the kid. I just don't like the kid liking my daughter."

"He's a great poker player."

"You say that like it's a positive thing."

"Isn't it? You always say a good poker player means someone with real smarts, not book smarts."

"Okay, look, maybe I said that once. But I want you to have every opportunity in life. I want you to be like your mother . . . to go to a fancy school and have a fancy life, with the best things money can buy."

"And what if I don't want that? What if I want to enter the World Series of Poker and live in Las Vegas?"

"That's your grandfather talking. Look, just listen to your old man, and if you won't stay away from Mark, at least don't get serious or anything."

"Don't worry so much, Dad."

"I can't help it. But don't tell anyone I'm such an old lady. It'll ruin my reputation." He winked at me.

"Wait till they hear down at the bar," I teased him. "There'll be no living it down. Blackjack King is actually a softie."

Dad came over to me and gave me a hug. "You know, Lulu, all my life I've been a tough guy, but the day you were born I just melted." He kissed the top of my head.

"Want to play a few hands, Dad?"

"Sure."

We got out the deck of cards and played some gin rummy, just the two of us. My favorite memories of my father, my whole life, have been nights spent until two or three in the morning playing cards. If I have a problem, it somehow makes me forget about it for a few hours. Sometimes I even think of the solution to my problem while being distracted by the cards. So I played rummy, lining up my hearts and spades and diamonds and clubs in my hand, until I figured out how Dack and I were going to get his grandfather's watch back.

Chapter Four

Lulu's Rule of Poker #4:
Never underestimate a female opponent.

Saturday night, Dad and I went to the bar to watch the fights. I know some people think boxing is a disgusting sport. Every time I have it on at Mom's apartment, she squeezes her eyes shut as she walks through the room. She once made the mistake of peeking when a cornerman was sticking a Q-tip into a cut above a boxer's eye—*way* into it. Like, the whole swab kind of disappeared, and blood was streaming down the guy's sweaty face. Mom nearly passed out.

But Dad loves the sport, and I'm so used to it, I don't even blink. The sight of blood doesn't bother me. In fact, thanks to Dad's obsession with boxing, I could have a career in surgery and never feel queasy a single day of my residency.

Dad and I sat side by side on bar stools, munching peanuts. Dad drank a beer; I drank Coke. When I was a little girl, my grandfather used to stick six maraschino cherries in all my sodas. When I got to be about ten or eleven, I decided maraschinos were the most disgusting fruit known to mankind. But I didn't have the heart to tell Grandpa. He still will stick one or two in, even though I'm way too old for them.

As we sat there watching two very large men punch each other bloody on the television, I waited for Mark to show up. Every time the bar door opened and a gust of air blew in, I turned around to see if it was him. Eventually Mark appeared.

He came over to me and said, "Hey, Lulu. I was hoping to see you here."

"Me, too." I hopped off my bar stool and maneuvered away from my father so he couldn't hear every single word of the conversation. Though he wasn't fooling me any. I could see Dad leaning in a little bit, trying to eavesdrop. Some tough guy. When it came to his only daughter and dating? He was clearly going to be worse than my mother.

"You want to get out of here for a little while? Maybe go get something to eat?" Mark asked.

The bar was crowded, and he was so close to me I could smell his cologne, which wasn't overpowering, but was sexy enough to make me want to stand even closer to him. Sometimes Angie and I go to Macy's and stand at the cologne counter smelling all the guys' scents. I think Mark was wearing Polo. In any case, he smelled . . . yummy.

"Sure."

Just then my grandfather signaled Mark from behind the bar.

"One sec, Lulu. Then we'll head over to this little Italian place I know, okay? Get some pizza or something?"

"Sure."

I watched as my grandfather and Mark talked. I couldn't hear a word they were saying. It was too loud. Mark came back a minute or two later, looking really depressed.

"What?" I asked him.

"Your grandfather needs me to do something for him. I have to go."

"Go?" I couldn't believe this. "Well, can I come with you for a while?"

"No, Lulu. Your grandfather wouldn't like that."

"Why?"

Mark looked away. "He just wouldn't."

Then I got it. "This has to do with gambling, doesn't it? He's got you running one of his errands for the football receipts he takes in." My dad and grandfather took in some illegal sports betting. Dad called it the Lulu College Fund—he set aside some of the money he made for my future.

"I can't say, Lulu," Mark said. "Please . . . don't ask me, okay?"

"Fine," I said, and crossed my arms.

He took his hand and tilted my chin up. "Listen . . . give me your e-mail and I'll write you. I'll see you next time you come down here. It's every other weekend, right?"

I nodded and told him my e-mail address. Then I gave him a hug—and could feel that his biceps were rock hard when he hugged me back. Wait until I told Angie all this. After Mark left, I looked from my grandfather to my father, then back again. They may have had poker faces, but I knew that it was a setup. My grandfather had sent Mark on the errand because my dad told him to. Well, it would take more than that to keep me from Mark.

The next day, Dad and I had breakfast at this real classic New York diner. The menu is as thick as the darn Bible, with huge pages splattered with old grease spots. We ordered eggs and hash browns and bacon and sausage and coffee and pretty much everything that is bad for you to eat for breakfast. This Sunday ritual with Dad is the polar opposite of my Sunday ritual with Mom. My mother is one of New York's "ladies who lunch," and I call what they do on Sunday the "B-words who brunch." She usually drags me to these ridiculously expensive brunches with smoked salmon and capers, jumbo shrimp, ice sculptures, a harpist, and all sorts of fancy foods. Those women can sit there and gossip for hours. Whatever. I like Sundays with Dad better.

After breakfast Dad drove me home. He pulled up in front of the building and shut off the bike. I took off my helmet and climbed off the motorcycle.

"Want to come up and say hi to Mom?"

"Nah. She'd probably give me a hard time because I let you stay up too late and you ate crap for breakfast."

"We could tell her I had organic yogurt and granola." My mother is one of those people who believes in feeding your brain the best food possible. She isn't convinced when I tell her I know my brain works better on hot dogs.

"Are you suggesting that we lie to your mother, Lulu?" my father asked in mock horror.

I stuck my hand on my hip. "Sure. Weren't you the one who told me to tell her I got that sunburn from a tanning bed, not from going to Vegas for the weekend last month?"

He winked at me. "Now, you know I love your mother. But ... well, she doesn't quite understand my world."

"I know."

"She still seeing Mr. Mayor?"

"Yeah." I rolled my eyes. "He wants me to spend some time with him—just me and him. Alone."

"Why?"

I shrugged. "Get to know me."

"Yeah. Well, you already have a dad. So even if he's getting serious with your mother, he'd better realize you're my girl."

Dad looked a little sad as he pulled me to him and kissed the top of my head.

"Dad?"

"Hmm?"

"Would it bother you if Mom got married again?"

"To the mayor?"

I nodded.

"A little. But listen, Lulu . . . I may not have gone to college, but I'm smart enough to know when there are two people who absolutely, positively shouldn't be together—and that's your mom and me. I love her. I'll always love her. But she's like one of those fancy little apartment dogs in a diamond collar, and I'm a pit bull."

"What does that make me? A mutt?"

He laughed, hugged me good-bye, started the bike back up, and drove away. I went inside, waved to the doorman on duty, and took the elevator up to my floor.

Mom wasn't home. She was obviously still out eating caviar with her pals in their Chanel suits. I dumped my backpack in my room and hopped into the shower. I was supposed to be at Dack's in an hour.

As soon as I stepped out of the shower, my hair immediately began curling into its usual wild state. It's hard to even pull a comb through it. I changed into a pair of jeans and an Abercrombie T-shirt and went into my room to check my e-mails. I had one from Mark. I couldn't believe he remembered my address—I hadn't written it down: PokerLuluKing972@ hotmail.com.

```
Hey, Lulu,

    How's the sexiest poker player in
New York? You know, I always win when
I'm around you. I think you're my lucky
charm. Call my cell sometime to talk.

    Mark
```

I wrote him back. Dad *did* say I could see him if I didn't get serious. Well, it's not like I was going to *marry* the guy.

```
Mark,

    There's no such thing as Lady Luck.
You're just a good poker player . . .
but I'm glad you win when I'm around.
I'll try to call you next time I'm at
my dad's.

    Lulu
```

I pressed send and felt a little thrill. I never felt that way around any of the guys at school. My mom says that since forever, women have loved bad boys. When she was my age, she had a crush on Sylvester Stallone in *Rocky*. She shut her eyes at all the fight scenes, but there's this scene in his disgusting apartment (and it's disgusting even by my dad's standards) where he kisses the girl he later marries. It's very hot. I guess my dad was her Rocky.

About fifteen minutes later, I left a note for my mom and took the elevator down to the lobby. Dack lives only four blocks from me. I walked over to his place, where the doorman there waved and sent me on up.

Mrs. Kensington opened the door. "Lulu." She smiled. "Good to see you."

Now, actually, I have to say that she didn't smile. Not really. She was freshly Botoxed, which meant she gave the smallest illusion of a smile, more like a tiny pulling back of her lips, letting you *think* she was smiling. But she wasn't really.

"Thanks. Is Dack home?"

"He's in his room. Maybe you can cheer him up. He's been a bear all weekend. Frankly, it's all his father's fault. I'm thinking of sending Dack to therapy.

45

Anyway, you go see him." She gave me her best Botox smile again and waved her hand in the direction of Dack's room. On her wrist hung this diamond tennis bracelet with round diamonds the size of marbles. As she had told me more than once, living well is the best revenge. For, like, the millionth time I was glad my parents got along. If the worst disagreement they had was over hot dogs for breakfast, I was pretty lucky.

I made my way through the immense apartment to Dack's room. He's a major gadget freak, so he has every kind of iPod, DVD, CD, computer, and network electronic device you can think of, not to mention tons of video games and game systems. However, his mom still had his room professionally decorated. Which meant it looked like George Washington should have slept there, with a big four-poster bed and heavy antique furniture. George Washington transplanted into the twenty-first century. George Washington with a PlayStation.

"You look terrible, Dack," I said as I flopped onto his bed.

"I know. I haven't slept since I lost the watch."

Dack's hands were shaking. He shut his bedroom door so his mother couldn't overhear us.

"Look, we're going to get it back. I have a plan."

"God, that's great. What?"

"Well, do you promise never to gamble with guys like that again?"

"I promise, swear . . . anything. What's your plan?"

"I'll win it back," I said confidently.

"Win it back?" Dack looked at me. "Do you think you can beat them? Like, for sure?"

I nodded. "Look, a lot of guys from tough neighborhoods play poker. They may even be pretty good. But they all make the same mistake when they play with me."

"What's that?"

"They assume because I'm a girl that I'm chicken at the table. They like to try to chase me—raise really big to see if I have the nerve to bet like a guy. Then I crush them when they find out that not only am I so *not* afraid to bet big . . . I'm also a really good player."

"But what if you get bad cards? What if you don't have any luck that night?"

"Don't even say it. A good poker player makes her own luck. Now, do you have the number for those guys?"

"We can call Carter. I have his cell phone number."

"Fine. Give it to me."

Dack recited the number, and I dialed.

"Hello . . . Carter?"

"Yeah?"

"This is Lulu King. You don't know me, but I'm a poker player . . . and Dack . . . uh, Dalton Kensington is my best friend. And I hear you won his watch in a game. I want a chance to win it back for him."

"Look, little girl, we play real poker. You even want a seat at the table, you have to come with a thousand in cash."

I tried not to let him hear the hesitation in my voice. "Fine. I'll come with that. But you come with the watch."

"No problem. I love fresh meat. Game is Thursday night. Eight o'clock at the usual place. Dalton knows where." With that, he hung up.

"Well?" Dack asked.

"We're in."

"Great."

"One small, tiny little problem."

"What?"

"I need a bankroll of a thousand."

"A thousand?" Dack winced. "God, Lulu, I'm already down six hundred dollars. If my mom ever discovers I took a thousand out of my savings . . . she'll devise whole new ways of torturing me. Like making me go to family therapy."

"Dack, it's the only way they'll let me sit in. I can get a couple of hundred, but I can't raise a thousand without asking my dad for it. And he definitely wouldn't be happy. I mean, gambling is okay in his book, but he wouldn't like the stakes. Not at my age."

Dack took a deep breath. "All right. What if you lose, though?" He was whining.

"Dack, don't say that. I won't lose."

"Okay. Besides, I guess losing a wad of cash isn't as big a deal as losing that watch."

"No, it isn't." I bit my lip. "That's what's worrying me." Something about this seemed too easy. Were they planning on cheating? I hated a cheat. My father had taught me all the slick ways someone could cheat in cards. I knew them all. So I'd be watching.

These guys didn't know who they were dealing with.

And if they thought they could beat me just because I was a girl, they were in for a big surprise.

Chapter Five

Lulu's Rule of Poker #5:
Always size up your opponent.

My mother is a very smart woman. She can tell you everything you ever wanted to know— and a lot of stuff you probably never wanted to know—about the Bauhaus movement in art, or about Vincent van Gogh chopping off his ear, or Georgia O'Keeffe's complex relationship with men. Mom is smart, yes. But she is the queen of the bad idea.

On Monday, the mayor's secretary called me to arrange for my "date" with the mayor. Her voice was haughty—like she was doing me a big favor by arranging an evening of sheer torture.

"How would Thursday evening at six work? He has a late-afternoon meeting, but then he can clear his schedule."

"Um . . . I have plans." As in, poker.

"All right, then . . . you know, young lady, that the mayor is a very busy man."

"I know." Young lady? Oh, for God's sake.

"Let's see . . . how would Wednesday night at eight be? I know that's perhaps a little late for dinner on a school night, but he has a cocktail reception at six. I'm certain we can get him out of there in time for dinner at eight. Would that work?"

I was free, but the thought of sitting across from the mayor of New York City in some get-to-know-me scheme made me want to jump out the window of our penthouse.

"Miss King? Would that work? Would Wednesday evening work?" His secretary sounded a little impatient. I imagined her sitting behind an enormous desk in Gracie Mansion, tapping her foot while the cursor on her computer screen blinked back at her.

Hmm? How about if I penciled him in for half

past never? I was thinking of ten different ways to say no, but my mouth said, "Yes. Sure."

So that was it. Me and the mayor were set for Wednesday. I told my mother when she got home from the museum that night.

"Wonderful, darling." She beamed.

"You so owe me."

"Oh, don't be like that, Lulu."

"Why? He's *your* boyfriend, not mine. And I already *have* a father."

"I know. Lulu, I would never try to do anything to harm your relationship with your father."

"Well, just as long as he knows I'm not one of the perfect Park Avenue princesses."

My mom smiled. "I don't think anyone would mistake you for that. You are an original. Just like your father."

"Thanks."

"Speaking of your dad, I was actually going to talk to you about something. Your father called me at work today."

Uh-oh, I thought. He never called her at work.

"He told me you've got a friend. Mark."

"Yeah, so?"

"Lulu . . . take it from a woman who knows: Bad

boys are intriguing. Sexy, even. But they're just not good for you."

"You sound like Dad. It's a guy, Mom, not a case of the flu."

"We just worry about you, Lulu."

"I think I'm smart enough to handle myself. I'm not you. It's not like I'll be eloping to Las Vegas. We're just friends."

"Tallulah Elizabeth King . . . there's no need to be so snide."

I rolled my eyes. "Sorry. Am I dismissed?"

"Fine. You're being rude."

"Fine," I snapped back. I turned around and retreated to my own room and flopped on my bed. I called Angie.

"Hey," she answered on the first ring.

"Hi. Just got in a fight with my mother."

"Over what?"

"Mark."

"Sexy tattooed boy?"

"Yeah."

"Lemme guess. She wants you dating a second or third, like Ralph."

"Exactly."

"She'll get over it."

"I guess so. I mean, what's the point of having divorced parents if they gang up on you?"

"Exactly. My mother has a restraining order out on my father."

"Really?"

"No, but man, can they fight. Still. Ten years after their divorce. They can't even sit together at parent-teacher night. Can't talk without ending up in a screaming match."

"Well, I wouldn't want that. But now they're both butting into my business."

I then told Angie all about Dack's mess.

"That boy had better steer clear of the card table."

"I think he's learned his lesson."

"Hope so. Or we'll just have to further his humiliation by getting him naked next time we play strip poker."

I laughed at the thought. Later, after I hung up and did my homework, I started mentally picturing the poker game. I needed to find out more about my opponents. That helps. You know their weaknesses. Like, Dack is totally sunk at the sight of a lacy bra. And this guy my dad plays with sometimes, Charley Aces—well, he insists people call him that, like he's some great player—but everyone knows he has this weird habit of scratching his head when he has a bad hand.

I needed to know what I was going to be up against. The next two days at school, I asked around. I found out Carter, who used to go to our school until he got busted for drugs, had a bad temper. I even found a guy besides Dack who'd lost to him before—a kid in my Latin class named Tobias.

Yes, Latin. I know, it's a dead language. Tell that to my Latin professor, who acts like we're really going to use it in life. Um, not unless Caesar rises from the grave. Anyway, Tobias, a third-generation Baxter Academy student—and a third himself, Tobias James Wilton III—told me, "Carter never checks to the raiser."

When someone checks, it means they're not necessarily interested in driving the pot up just for the sake of doing so. They may figure their hand isn't that good—or they may be trying to make you *think* their hand isn't that good. Either way, Carter never checks. It means he always raises.

"He never folds, either."

"Really?" I asked.

Tobias nodded.

"Anything else?"

"If he has a good hand, he chatters more. You know, like mocking the other guys at the table. Egging them on."

"Thanks, Tobias."

"One more thing."

"Hmm?"

"I *really* hate that guy, so do me a favor and *fabricati diem*."

Which means "make my day" in Latin.

I laughed out loud—which earned me a dirty look from our Latin teacher—and gave Tobias my biggest smile ever. "Sure thing. You know what they say . . . *Maior risus, acrior ensis*."

The bigger the smile, the sharper the knife.

Chapter Six

Lulu's Rule of Poker #6:
Sometimes you have to lay all your cards on the table.

The mayor sent a long, shiny black stretch limo with black-tinted windows for me on Wednesday. I spent a half hour picking out my outfit. I mean, precisely what do you wear to a get-to-know-Mom's-boyfriend dinner? Add to that the fact that he's the mayor and I was majorly freaked. I ended up picking a pair of black velvet jeans and a really cute gray cashmere sweater that my mom bought me for Christmas last year.

At 7:45—precisely, not 7:44 or 7:46—his security

detail buzzed up to the apartment and announced they were here.

"Have fun, darling." Mom squeezed me as I was putting on my coat.

"Fun?" I looked at her. "I'd rather take advanced Latin next year. Better yet, I'd rather take Latin all summer in summer school than do this."

"Oh, please . . . please . . . just try. For me?"

"Let me rephrase that. I'd rather major in Latin in college than do this."

"Lulu," she pleaded, dragging out my name, like, *LuuuuuuuuuuuLuuuuuuuuuuuuuu.*

"Don't worry. I'll be nice. And then when I'm older I can go to therapy and complain about you." She hates when I say that. Mostly because nearly everyone in Mom's social circle sees a shrink of some sort. Mom doesn't. She's very practical. She doesn't need one. Though maybe she does, considering this stupid idea of me getting to know Mr. New York. "I'm just kidding, Mom. It'll be fine."

Of course, *fine* is a relative term.

When I got downstairs, the mayor's security detail said hello, and the two main guys introduced themselves as they helped me into the limousine. There was an unmarked security car in front of the limo, and one behind it.

The security guys looked like Secret Service or cops, right down to little earpieces in their ears. The mayor paid for some of his own security. He was a millionaire several hundred times over, and there had once even been rumors of him being a target as a symbol of New York. These bodyguards were clearly professionals. It almost felt like *I*, Lulu King, was a superstar. But then I quickly came back to earth. These were football player–sized men hired to babysit me.

"We're meeting him at the restaurant," said one particularly ginormous man named Duncan.

"Where are we going?"

"You have reservations at Pandora's."

Inwardly I groaned. New York City is a place of too many restaurants to count. You can get any kind of food, anytime, day or night: Thai, Chinese, Japanese, Italian, American, French, Indian, Polynesian, Russian, Brazilian. If it is a country and it has food, chances are you can find a restaurant for that cuisine. Pandora's is one of those New York "institutions," meaning superexpensive and superfancy. The kind of place where you have to worry about what fork you're using. My mom loves it there. My father wouldn't be caught dead entering its doors.

The limousine pulled away from the curb. Was something wrong with a good hot dog? Or even a Broadway play? If we went to a play, then I wouldn't have to worry about thinking up clever things to talk about.

"There's soda in the bar," the chauffeur told me. "And the controls to the TV and the stereo back there are on that remote next to your the seat. Is the temperature comfortable?"

"Yeah. I'm fine."

"The seats are even heated," he said.

Just what I needed. A warm rear end.

We snaked through traffic and arrived at the building for Pandora's, which is on the top floor of a huge skyscraper with views of the whole city. When you're standing on the sidewalk, you can't even really see the top, no matter how far back you crane your neck. I rode up in a brass-and-glass elevator to the penthouse, along with Thing One and Thing Two— extremely burly security men.

The mayor was waiting for me by the coat-check area. "Lulu." He smiled and leaned in and kissed my cheek. He was wearing his trademark dark blue suit, power tie, and lucky four-leaf-clover tie tack. Three bodyguards stood near him, too.

"Hi, David." I smiled. Sort of. Maybe it was a grimace.

"You don't like this place?"

"No, it's fine. Great." I tried to sound enthusiastic. But they were piping in opera.

"I can tell you're not excited. You know, I asked my secretary where she would want to go for a quiet dinner, and she suggested here. But she's also fifty-five years old. Ancient!" He laughed.

"This is fine."

"No. You want hip? We can go hip."

Hip? Who was he kidding?

"Would you rather go to Nobu? Or back to Gracie Mansion? I could have one of the chefs prepare you whatever you want."

I shrugged. The two beefy bodyguards who'd ridden up in the elevator with me were looking at me. Actually, now that I glanced around, most of the restaurant was staring.

"Come here." David motioned. The snooty maître d', with his tuxedo and a pinched appearance as if he had something in his pants, looked down his nose at me. I would have given anything to be in the back room at King's Pub playing poker.

I moved closer to David, and he lowered his voice to almost a whisper. "If we're going to be friends, Lulu, real friends, then let's be honest with each other."

I gazed directly at him. His blue eyes looked like he really meant it.

Sometimes, in poker and in life, you have to lay all your cards on the table.

"Honestly?" I said to him.

"Yes. Honestly. Would you rather go somewhere else?"

I exhaled. "I'd rather go anywhere else than here."

"How about we see the real New York together?"

I looked at him skeptically.

"Come on." He grabbed my hand and motioned to his security detail. Next thing I knew, we were riding back down the elevator. When we got to the street he walked over to one of his bodyguards.

"Do we still have all that Yankee stuff in the back?"

"Yes, Mr. Mayor."

"Do me a favor and open the trunk."

The guy took the keys out of the engine and popped up the trunk. I peered in.

"Holy cow!" Inside the trunk was practically a sporting goods store of jerseys and T-shirts and baseball caps.

"Sometimes"—the mayor looked at me—"I'm in a rush and I have to go throw out the first pitch at Yankees stadium, or I have to go to a lunch celebrating the NYPD." He moved aside a Yankees jersey and there was a neatly folded New York Police Department sweatshirt. "So my secretary—though she did come up with the very bad idea of taking you to a far too boring restaurant—came up with the very *good* idea of storing all this stuff in the trunk of one of the security detail cars. That way, no matter where I am, if I need an 'I love New York' change of clothes, I've got it."

I grinned. "And so what does this have to do with not eating at some ridiculously overpriced and overhyped restaurant?"

"My darling Lulu, we are about to blend in."

Then the mayor of New York City—one of the most powerful men in the United States (he was, after all, a zillionaire, too)—started taking off his suit jacket. He took off his tie, unbuttoned his shirt, and tossed on a blue New York Yankees sweatshirt. He messed up his hair a bit, threw on a baseball cap, and handed me one, too.

"You *do* like the Yankees, don't you?"

I smiled at him. "Come on . . . I couldn't be a real New York girl if I didn't."

"All right, then, now we can go have some fun."

He told the extra security detail to go home. Then, in just one car—not the big stretch limo either, but a plain unmarked Ford—we set out to see New York.

"Hungry?" he asked me as we settled into the backseat.

"Starving."

"Archie," he said to the driver, "how about finding us a hot-dog cart?"

"Now you're talking." I smiled at him.

We drove through the streets, ending up taking a turn through Central Park. It's always been an oasis. When people call New York a concrete jungle, they mean it. But Central Park is lush and green. In fall its colors are vivid reds and oranges. In winter there's a skating rink. We did find a vendor at an exit from the park, a blue umbrella above his stainless-steel cart.

The mayor hopped out, pulled his cap down low, and bought us two hot dogs with extra relish and mustard and two cans of Coke. He motioned to me to get out of the car. The two of us started walking over by the Plaza, and talking. I was amazed how no one really noticed us. We looked like two tourists who happened to like the Yankees. I kind of liked the feeling that I was doing something secretive and fooling all the passersby.

A few feet behind us the two remaining security guys walked. But they were far enough back that David and I could talk in private.

"So . . . your mother tells me you like Latin class."

I looked over at him, nearly choking on my hot dog. "You're kidding!"

"Yeah, I am." He started laughing. "You know, I went to a school like Baxter. My parents were convinced I would learn everything I needed to know to . . . I don't know, run for president one day. But I have to be honest."

I looked at him intently.

"I learned a lot more from the year I took off and backpacked through Europe on my own."

"You didn't go with a friend?"

He shook his head. "I think I learned so much precisely because I was alone. It forced me to be outgoing, make friends from all over the world. Break out of my comfort zone. It was a great experience. But don't tell your mother I said that. I'm sure she wouldn't like the idea of you bypassing college."

"No. She has her heart set on me going off to Vassar or the Sorbonne."

"*Très bien*," he said in perfect French. "Well, anyway, it was a wonderful year for me. And when I returned, I started my first company."

The mayor's story was legendary. He started trading stocks and bonds and eventually became this whiz-kid financial guru. Then a hedge fund king.

"As long as we're being open," I said, "can I ask you something?"

"Anything."

"How come you've never been married?"

"I never met the right woman. I met a lot of terrific women. Brainy, beautiful. But . . . well, they were kind of like this hot dog here." He held out the last bit of his dog. "A lot of filler."

"I don't get it."

"Well, on the outside, on paper, they were perfect. But I didn't find the heart I was looking for."

"So you're comparing women to pig parts?" I said teasingly.

"Well . . . not exactly, Lulu. You know, you sound like some of my political opponents."

"I'm just kidding. It's just that, if you can have any woman in all of New York, why not some . . . you know, young hottie? Why my mom? Why someone with a kid my age?"

"Because she's who I fell in love with. And—"

"And you're stuck with me as part of the package."

"I don't see it that way at all. I wanted to spend time alone with you so we can have a real friendship. I know you're very close with your father, and I would never try to break that bond. But I love your mother, and you love your mother, and that gives us something really special in common."

We crossed the street, where a long line of hansom cabs stood, their horses whinnying in the night air.

"Want to go for a ride? Come on. . . . It's very New York, Lulu."

"Sure."

"Pick a chariot, my lady."

I walked down the line of horse-drawn carriages

and their drivers. I spotted a beautiful chestnut-colored horse with braids in her mane and a white star in her coat right above her eyes. She was beautiful.

"How about that one?" I pointed.

"Perfect," he said.

We climbed into the horse-drawn carriage. The driver gave us a tip of his black silk top hat, but he didn't look like he recognized the mayor. The horse clip-clopped through the park, and we pulled a tartan-plaid wool blanket onto our laps.

"I love New York," he said. "I make more money just running my company. But I think this is the greatest city in the world in the greatest country in the world, and I love it. I love the Yankees. Don't tell the Mets fans that. I love the New York Giants—even though they play in Jersey. I love the hot dogs and the pretzels. I love the museums—something your mom and I have in common. I like how there's always people around. Always energy. A feeling. It's not like anywhere else on earth."

"Me, too," I said. "Dad takes me to Vegas a lot. And we always have a great time. We stay at the best hotels, stay up late, see all the shows—I love Cirque du Soleil. He spoils me. But there's something about landing back in Kennedy airport that lets me know I'm home. The minute I see the sky-line, I just relax."

"It's in your blood. For real New Yorkers, they can travel the globe, but they'll always have the city as part of them." He was quiet a moment. "Let me ask you something, Lulu."

"Okay."

"Could you ever see yourself living in Gracie Mansion?"

Oh, my God, it was true what Page Six said. He was thinking of giving my mother a huge diamond and asking her to marry him. Supposedly a Page Six spy had spotted him at Cartier. And some other Page Six scoop hound had said the city's most famous pri-vate jeweler had "paid a secret visit to Gracie Man-sion." I wanted to throw myself under the horse's hooves.

"In Gracie Mansion?" I squeaked.

"Yeah. It's full of history. Beautiful. It's part of New York. Part of the city."

"To be honest, it's not Gracie Mansion that I wouldn't like. I mean, not the building, you know. It would be living in a fishbowl. You and Mom are photographed every time you go somewhere. Do you know there's even a blogger who rates my mother's outfits? Some society blog. Kind of like the fashion police. Not only that, but you have to have a security detail." I looked over my shoulder, and sure enough, two burly guys were taking a ride in a horse and carriage behind us.

The mayor looked disappointed. "But if we worked at it, I mean . . . tried really hard to become a family . . . not replacing your father or anything like that, but being our own little family, don't you think it might be fun?"

I shrugged. But as I looked out at the New York night into Central Park, its trees hanging over us and making it dark, all I could think was that no, it didn't sound like fun at all.

Chapter Seven

Lulu's Rule of Poker #7:
Sometimes luck is on your side.

After my "date" with the mayor, my mother pumped me for information when I got upstairs.

"Well? How did it go?"

"Okay." I mean, was I supposed to say it ranked with the time I saw Green Day in concert? No . . . it ranked more with the time my great-aunt Charlotte took me to *Cats*.

"Well, what did he say? And what did you end up ordering for dinner?"

"We actually got some hot dogs."

"Hot dogs?"

I nodded. "His secretary made the reservations. Mom . . . the restaurant she picked was so boring. So we just left Pandora's and did our own thing."

"You mean to tell me the mayor of New York wanted to take you to a veritable institution for dinner, let you order whatever you want, including the two-hundred-dollar lobster tails flown in from South Africa, and you opted for a hot dog?"

"Yes. But we did take a horse-and-carriage ride through Central Park," I offered, as I could tell my mother was likely gearing up for a migraine.

"Well, what did you talk about?"

I shrugged. "You know, he asked me how I would feel about the three of us becoming a family of some sort."

Mom looked pleased. "Really? How did he say it?"

I sighed. She was worse than Lydia Manchester, whose pathetic lovesickness for Dack is legendary. Dack, unfortunately for poor Lydia, does not return the affection. In fact, he has despised her since second grade, when she told the entire class she saw him eat boogers—which wasn't true, but somehow she thought this would make him like her.

"Mom . . . what is your problem? You're acting totally weird."

"It's not weird. Is it so wrong that I would want you to get along with David?"

"No. But the more important thing is that *you* get along with him. He's not my new best friend, but he is very nice."

"Lulu . . . can't you at least try to warm up to the idea of us?"

"Mom, I'm not you. I don't *want* a socialite's life—fancy parties and the ladies who lunch. I am just as happy with hot dogs as lobster, and I really wouldn't want to live in Gracie Mansion." I turned around and went to my room and shut the door. I had never seriously thought about what would happen if either of my parents got remarried. Mom always seemed too busy with her charity work and her career. And Dad? Well, Dad was Dad. He was a totally awesome father, but as a boyfriend, as far as I could see from the women he dated, he sucked. He never remembered to call when he said he would. And he'd ditch any date for a good poker game. As he put it, "Lulu, I tried the marriage thing once—that's enough for me. You're my girl."

I got undressed, went into my bathroom, washed

up, and brushed my teeth. Climbing into bed, I tried to envision the game tomorrow. I wasn't intimidated. When you've played poker downtown with guys who break legs for a living, or who are missing a few teeth, or have tattoos of chopped-off heads on their biceps, a few pretty boys playing with Daddy's money aren't so scary at all.

The next night Dack and I showed up at some guy named Chip's apartment. Chip? How many tough guys do you know named Chip? Apparently this was a standing Thursday-night game. I had told my mother I was going to a study session, and as luck would have it, she was going with the mayor to a black-tie function, which meant she wouldn't be home before two in the morning—it was all the way in Greenwich, Connecticut, at the mansion of some guy who owned a major brokerage house. All I had to do was be home before two and I had it made. Well, that and win the watch back.

Dack fidgeted the whole way up in the elevator. He wasn't going to play—he was supposed to be going with me purely for moral support. He told his mom that he was staying over at my house because my mom was going to be out super late and that way we could study in peace and I wouldn't have to feel so scared being alone in my huge apartment. For the record, you would need to be the crew from *Ocean's Eleven* to break into my apartment building, but his mother bought it. Yes, we're a little old for "sleepovers," but my mom and his mom know that we're like brother and sister. The thought of even kissing Dack would make me burst out laughing— and he feels the same. So when his mom travels or my mom has some sort of conflict, very often we do stay over at each other's places.

"Stop fidgeting. You're making me nervous."

"I'm sorry. I'm just really worried about the watch."

"Well, getting me all uptight isn't going to help matters. And when we get in there, don't hover over the game. Go watch TV or make a sandwich. I don't know. Just don't hang over me."

We knocked on the door to Chip's apartment— it was on the Upper East Side, an old building with gargoyles and fancy stone on the outside, and marble floors and expensive paintings in the hallways on the inside. A guy with a short, gelled-back haircut and a rich-boy sneer opened the door. I saw Carter behind him—wearing Dack's watch.

"Well . . . if it isn't two more chumps for our game. Come on in." Carter smiled.

I grinned back at him—a fake grin. I was so going to love taking him down.

Dack and I walked into the place. Chip's family was obviously loaded, as they had two floors—a spiral staircase wound up to the second floor. Whereas my mom decorates in French country, and it seems kind of homey, this guy's family decorator must have been from Mars. It was supermodern, and I felt like I had boarded a spacecraft. There were things in the middle of the floor. I couldn't tell if they were sculptures or chairs.

"Want a beer? Something to drink?" Chip asked.

"No, thanks." I'd never drink alcohol at the table. And in all honesty, if you spend enough time around a bar, like I do at my grandfather's place, you see a lot of messy drunks. Keg parties and getting blind drunk just have no appeal for me.

"Follow me."

Chip led the way through the spacecraft—um, apartment.

"Here's food. Help yourself." he motioned to a buffet table loaded with sushi and chips and several gourmet pizzas. "Over there is the TV, pool table, general hangout area." He looked at Dack. "You can hang there, if you want. And over here"—he gestured to a room off of the TV room—"is the game."

He introduced me to the other guys. The players were Chip, me, Carter, some college guy from NYU named Mitch, and some weird older guy. He said his name was Al, and he looked about thirty. Well dressed. I couldn't figure out what he was doing playing with a bunch of teenagers, but whatever. There were a few girls sitting in the den area with some other guys, watching MTV on a plasma-screen.

I sat down. "What's the game?"

"Five-card stud. Jacks or better. Progressive," Chip said. He wore a white T-shirt and a tie with playing cards all over it slung around his neck. A lot of players wear lucky clothing, including Dack. A lot of good that did him.

Okay, so here's how "jacks or better" works. Everyone antes. That means you stick the basic bet in the middle of the table. Let's say that's ten bucks. Everyone gets five cards facedown. You pick up your cards and look at them. If in your hand you have a pair of jacks or better, you can open. If no one at the table has a pair of jacks or better—which is actually pretty common, since there aren't any wild cards—

everyone folds, meaning you all give your cards back to the dealer. The dealer shuffles and deals all over again. You ante in *again*. Then next time you have to have queens or better. Same thing. If no one has better than that, you turn in your cards, redeal, and ante in *again*. Only this time it's kings or better. Then aces or better. Then back down to jacks or better, each time anteing until someone can open. Then it progresses like regular five-card stud. Needless to say, the pot can get pretty big.

"What's the ante?" I asked.

"Twenty bucks. Only when we go next round, the ante is forty. Then sixty. Eighty. You get the idea."

Of course I did. This game wasn't for chickens. They were going to see if I had the stomach for it.

"Deal me in, boys." I smiled.

"When it's just you and me left at the table," Carter said, "we bet the watch. If you last that long."

"Don't worry about me. What if you're out before then?"

Carter smiled coldly. "Not a chance."

Dack started pacing. He was making me nervous. "Go watch TV and get something to eat," I snapped at him.

With Dack gone, Carter dealt the cards. There

was the usual banter between players. I looked at the clock on the mantel. It was eight. I had less than five hours, give or take, to get that watch back. I had to bet aggressively but smart.

The first to fall was the weird old guy. He had been bugging me anyway, asking all sorts of questions. I assumed he was trying to get me off my game. He even asked where I learned to play.

"My dad. Blackjack King. He taught me from when I was really little. I learned the hands of poker before I learned the multiplication tables."

"Well"—he winked at me—"I hope you let me have a rematch sometime."

"Sure."

"I figured you weren't from around here. I mean, these trust-funders—you're a little more card savvy than that."

"My mom is from uptown; my dad is downtown. She even dates the mayor, of all things."

"Ever play him?"

I shook my head. "He's not the type."

Next to fall was Chip. Then Mitch.

At 11:15, it was just me and Carter. Then my cell phone rang.

"Hold on," I said before the cards were dealt.

Caller ID told me it was my mother. I had Dack sit at my spot to watch my chips—I didn't trust these guys—and I went into the bathroom, where she wouldn't hear people in the background.

"Hello?"

"Hi, honey, just checking on you. We're leaving Connecticut now. I guess we'll be home in an hour or two. Just wanted to say good night."

"Night, Mom."

"David says he had a great time with you. Thanks so much for going. It meant a lot to me. I'm sorry if I was a little overbearing about it. I'm so lucky to have a daughter like you. Not an ounce of trouble."

And at that precise moment, someone banged on the bathroom door. "I gotta pee!" he said.

"What was that?"

"Nothing. TV. Mom, I'm really tired. I'll talk to you in the morning." At that I hung up the phone before some other idiot tried to barge in on me.

I left the bathroom as my cell phone rang again. I let it go to voice mail. I needed to get that watch back. And fast. If I knew my mother, that limo she went to Greenwich in was now doing ninety miles per hour on its way back to Manhattan, with her telling the chauffeur to step on it.

I returned to the poker table feeling like I'd been kicked in the gut. I didn't like lying to my mom to begin with—even if it *was* for a good reason, to help Dack. And the idea that I might get *caught* in a lie was even worse.

"Okay, little lady," Carter said when I sat back down. "Looks like we're pretty evenly matched."

I nodded. We each had about the same amount of chips in front of us.

"So here's the game," Carter said. "Five-card stud. Three hands. Best two out of three takes the watch."

Considering I was pressed for time, this sounded okay. But—and this was a big *but*—I didn't like those odds. I was going to need all the luck in the universe to pull this off.

The first hand I was dealt a pair of threes. Not exactly a stellar hand. I lost. He had a full house—eights over twos. Enough to beat me.

The second hand I was dealt four clubs and a diamond. I was one card away from a flush—all the same suit. One card. But then, I had only one chance when I traded in that single card. I wanted to throw up.

I traded in my card and got . . . a club. Carter had three of a kind—nines. I won.

So now, with thoughts of my mother freaking me out, it was time for the last hand. For the watch. Or, as my Dad says, "For all the marbles." As if anyone plays for marbles.

I picked up my five cards all at once. I purposely kept my face completely stoic. Stone-faced. I couldn't believe it. I had a straight to the queen—an eight, nine, ten, jack, queen. This was good. I held my breath and glanced at Carter. When it came time to ask for cards, he didn't trade in any either. So he was keeping all his cards. And I was keeping all mine. That meant he had a good hand, too.

"Okay, there, poker princess, show your cards."

I spread my straight down on the card table, fanning them out up to the queen.

Carter's expression grew dark. He angrily ripped the watch off his wrist. "You win." He didn't turn over his cards, though—and it's not in the rules that you have to. So I would never know how badly (or closely) I had beaten him.

Dack was beyond excited. He swooped his hand down and took the watch.

"Thanks, guys." I said. "Good game."

I reached my hand out, but Carter wouldn't take it. A total sore loser. I shrugged and got up. Dack and I left the apartment. He had the watch on his wrist.

"You staying at my house?" I asked. He had told his mother he was keeping me company until my mother got home and would stay over, so I guessed it was best that we stuck to our original story.

"Yeah. But during school tomorrow, I'm going to leave the watch at your place. I'm terrified of anything happening to it now."

"Check to make sure it's really your watch."

"What? You think they'd make a switch?"

"Just check, will you?"

He slid it off his wrist and flipped it over, and there on the back was JFK's inscription. "It's my watch." He sighed in relief.

"Good." The elevator doors opened onto the lobby. "We've got to hurry, Dack. My mom called my cell. If I'm caught out this late on a school night, I'm toast."

The doorman hailed us a cab, and we raced back to my apartment. I hurriedly wrote my mother a note:

Mom:

Dack slept over. We were working late on a school project. Hope you had fun.

Love you,
Lulu

I prayed she would think the pounding on the bathroom door she heard was just Dack. Not that Dack is ever that crude, but maybe she just heard a male voice and not the whole "I gotta pee" thing.

Dack and I changed into sweats and T-shirts, and I crawled into bed. He blew up the air mattress and grabbed the sleeping bag he and Angie borrow when they stay over.

I turned off the light. In the darkness he said, "Thanks for saving my butt, Lulu. I owe you one, big-time."

"Dack?"

"Huh?"

"Remember the time my dad was in that motor-cycle accident and we didn't know how bad it was at first?"

"Yeah."

"And remember how queasy I got at the sight of blood, and me being terrified when I first saw him?" I mean, a boxing match is one thing, but this was my *dad*.

"Uh-huh," he whispered.

"Well . . . remember how you held my hand and never left my side the whole time? And how your mom came to the hospital with takeout from Peter Luger Steak House?"

"Only my mom brings three-hundred-dollar takeout, instead of McDonald's."

"Well . . . anyway, you don't owe me anything, Dack. That's what friends are for."

"Night, Lulu."

"Night."

When we woke up for school the next morning, Mom never said a word. She looked at us a little weirdly, and I caught her counting the bottles in the liquor cabinet later that day, but she never said anything.

I was home free.

Or so I thought.

Chapter Eight

Lulu's Rule of Poker #8:
When you're on a roll, go for it.

The next day, after school, my cell phone rang. I didn't recognize the phone number.

"Lulu? It's Mark."

First I won back the watch; now Mark called. And it wasn't even my dad's weekend, so I totally wasn't expecting to hear from him! I wondered if my horoscope was going to tell me this was my lucky week.

"Hey, Mark."

"Listen . . . I know it's not your weekend with

your dad, but I was wondering if maybe you wanted to meet tomorrow and do something."

"Sure. Like what?"

"Well," he said, "usually I say things like shoot pool or grab something to eat, but as it is I know your father doesn't like the idea of me hanging out with you. So I'm going to go crazy here and say let's go to a museum. Isn't your mom, like . . . in a museum or something? Like a painter?"

I tried not to giggle. "No. She's stuffed. She's in the Museum of Natural History."

"Come on. Give a guy a break, Lulu," he pleaded.

"No. She's not *in* a museum. She's a curator. She puts collections together."

"Okay, Miss Smarty-pants. Still . . . do you want to go to a museum? We can look at stuffed relatives of yours, or paintings, or whatever you want to go look at. You can teach me about art."

"Sounds great." Inside I wanted to scream—with happiness. We made plans to meet the next day at the Metropolitan Museum of Art. I know it like the back of my hand and decided we would look at the Goya exhibit—my mother's specialty—and then artists of the Renaissance.

Of course, a tiny little voice inside my head *also* wondered what my parents would think of this. As far as I was concerned, it wasn't like I was going to marry Mark. We were spending the day together. On the other hand, I've always gotten along with both my parents pretty well, and the idea of totally going against them didn't make me happy. Especially Dad, because, I admit it, I've always been his little girl. If I went, I'd be telling more lies. Sort of like the poker game. Suddenly I was keeping stuff from them.

But Mark was so hot.

Dack came over that night to collect his watch.

"Put it in a safe, and don't even take it out again until you're ready to give it to your grandkids," I told him.

"No problem."

"And no more gambling."

"I learned my lesson."

The two of us watched TV. I wasn't sure why, but I didn't tell him about my date with Mark for the next day. It's not that Dack likes me. I just wondered if he would be sort of like my parents—wanting me to stick to guys from Baxter.

––––––

The next day I spent an hour deciding what to wear, settling on Abercrombie jeans and a low-cut angora sweater. I put on my jean jacket and headed toward the door.

"Where are you going?" Mom asked.

"To the museum. I want to go to the Goya exhibit."

"Ding, ding, ding, ding, ding."

"What's that?"

"My BS meter. It's going off."

"Mom!" I said. My mother never cursed. That was Dad's department. I think the raciest she ever got was, "Darn!"

"Look, I'm not saying that you aren't culturally aware, because you are. But the Goya exhibit? On a Saturday? When you could be sleeping until two in the afternoon? Or at the very least not changing out of your pajamas. For that matter, your outfit looks suspiciously like a date outfit."

I decided right then I wasn't going to lie. "Fine. I'm meeting Mark at the Goya exhibit."

"Does your father know?"

"No, but let me guess—you're going to tell him."

"Lulu . . . first of all, though your father and I

may be divorced, you know perfectly well we communicate. We're not like Dack's parents, at each other's throats. We're both concerned about you and the choices you make. I don't keep things from him."

This I knew all too well, like the time I brought home an F on my geometry test—I despise math. Mom called Dad, and I had a tutor faster than you can say, "Toto, I don't think we're in Kansas anymore."

"Fine," I said as nonchalantly as I could. "Tell him."

"Lulu, it seems to me that if your father doesn't want you dating Mark, he must have a very important reason. I don't think that boy's a good influence. You know, you may soon be the future stepdaughter of the mayor of New York City. You have to think how things look."

My mouth dropped open, and I managed to stammer, "Wh-a-a-t?"

"Well, Lulu, please, honey. Be reasonable."

"You know, Mom . . . you've been hanging around with those stuck-up ladies who lunch for too long. The mom I know may be from the society pages, but she was wild enough to go to Vegas with my dad for one crazy weekend. I can't believe you're being like this. I'm outta here."

I turned around and left, slamming the apartment door behind me. When I got downstairs I decided to walk to the museum to cool off. I felt tears stinging my eyes—and since I had put on a little mascara (and not waterproof!), I didn't want to get all upset. By the time I got to the Met I was feeling better. I had calmed down, even though I still felt hurt.

I scanned the people on the sidewalk, and there he was, looking amazing in jeans, a black wool sweater, and a leather jacket. I waved, and he smiled at me and walked over and gave me a hug.

"Hey, Lulu."

"Hi."

"All right, so I'm a museum virgin. You're going to have to teach me everything. I don't know a thing. I think modern art looks like a monkey painted it. And as for the rest of it, I never know what I'm supposed to be seeing or what the artist is supposedly trying to say."

I smiled at him. "See . . . that's where you're wrong."

"What? Monkeys really *do* paint modern art?"

"No," I said. The wind whipped my hair in front of my face, but before I could move my hair out of my eyes, he used his hand to brush it back. I felt like my knees were going to give out. I exhaled. "No . . . it's that too many people run away from the arts for that exact reason. Critics make people feel dumb when it comes to art, or the symphony, or whatever."

"I do feel dumb. I'm breaking out in a sweat just at the thought of going in there." He grinned at me.

"But you shouldn't be intimidated by art. Art is another way of communicating. And yeah, maybe on one level the artist is saying something that the critics talk about. But on another level art is supposed to speak to you. It's about what talks to your heart or makes you angry or sad or moves you. You ever listen to Beethoven's Ninth?"

"Yeah. Sure. All the time. Wedged in between Green Day and the Killers on my iPod." He took my hand as we started up the steps and into the museum.

"Well, I love Green Day, too. And Springsteen. And Beck. And the Scissor Sisters. And Lou Reed. And a ton of music. But I also like Beethoven's Ninth. And when I hear it . . ." Suddenly I felt like a complete and total dork, so I shut up. "Never mind."

"No, no." He squeezed my hand. "Tell me."

"Well . . . sometimes I feel like I'm flying when I hear it."

"Flying?"

I nodded.

"If it can make you feel like you're flying, then I want to hear it," he said, smiling at me.

"It's the same thing with art. I can tell you all about Goya, and the Flemish portrait artists, and Degas, and Michelangelo. But in the end you have to look at it all and feel it and see what you like."

"I've never met anyone like you before. You can throw down a full house and at the same time tell me all about a bunch of dead guys' paintings."

His voice was totally sincere. My heart pounded. No guy had ever said anything like that to me, ever. In fact, no guy had ever known the two sides of my life except Dack. None of the Baxter guys would ever understand my father and me and my life in my grandfather's pub.

"Well, I never met anyone who was interested in full houses and inside straights . . . *and* learning about dead guys' paintings," I said back. "I think it's really cool you wanted to come here with me today."

We entered the museum. The Metropolitan Museum of Art's ceilings seem to go to heaven itself. It's huge, and people's hushed talking echoes throughout the exhibitions.

"Come on," I said, pulling his hand. "Let's go see some Renaissance dead guys."

The two of us laughed. Then we walked and talked until my voice was hoarse and my feet ached. We saw sculptures—including *The Thinker*—and ballerinas painted by Degas. We saw Goya's paintings of the Spanish Revolution, and a couple from his period of madness. We wandered through the antiquities exhibits. Mark held my hand the whole time, and I felt totally relaxed in between noticing my stomach doing flip-flops.

Finally it was getting near five o'clock.

"Want to get something to eat?" he asked.

"I'd better call my mom. She'll be worried."

Once we got outside on the stone steps, I called her. She answered on the first ring.

"I'm going to eat," I said.

"No. Did you forget tonight is the dinner party at Grandfather's?"

I groaned. "I totally spaced it out."

"Well, you know how he feels about his charities, darling. We have to be there." Then she was silent. I could tell she was mad.

"I'll be there. And I'm sorry about today."

"Me, too."

"I don't want to fight."

"Me either."

"I'll be home in a half hour."

"See you in a bit, then."

I closed my phone. "I have to get going. I forgot that I have this thing at my grandfather's." I rolled my eyes. "I love him, but he's on the board of fifteen different charities. I end up at all these black-tie events." I didn't mention that my grandfather was always trying to fix me up with New York's social registry.

Mark faced me and pulled me close to him. "I had a great time today."

"Me, too."

"And for the record? I like the guy who painted the animals with the moon."

"Rousseau."

"Yeah, him . . . You're the best art teacher a guy could have." He leaned in and kissed me. It was perfect—sexy, not too gentle, not too hard. "I'd go to a museum with you anytime, Lulu."

I stood on tiptoe and hugged him. Then he kissed me again. I shivered a little. He was the most amazing kisser, and I felt so lucky to find a guy—not a Baxter Academy guy, who acted like my dad's downtown life wasn't good enough—who liked the two sides to me.

We stood there kissing on the steps of the Met for a few minutes. I didn't want to go home. Reluctantly, I pulled back from him.

"I'd better get a cab," I whispered.

"Can I ask you something?"

"Sure."

"Are your parents upset . . . you know . . . that I called you?"

"Well . . ." I didn't know what to say. "I think they worry a little. But I'll tell them you're a nice guy. Who happens to like Rousseau."

"Well, don't go falling for any fancy rich boys tonight, okay?"

"Not a chance." I kissed him again, then ran down the steps and got a cab. Without a doubt, this was the best day of my life.

Chapter Nine

Lulu's Rule of Poker #9:
Forget what I said in Rule #7. Luck is an illusion.

When I got home, my mother had already laid out one of my gowns on my bed. The midnight blue velvet one.

I hurriedly brushed my teeth, brushed fresh mascara on my eyelashes, slid a lip gloss across my lips, and then looked at my hair. It was a mess, windblown and sloppy. I pulled it up in a high ponytail, threw a black velvet scrunchie around it, stuck two rhinestone combs in the sides of my hair, and put in small diamond drop earrings. By the time I pulled on my evening gown, I looked, as my mom put it, "presentable."

At seven a limousine picked us up for the ride to Grandfather's. He and my dad's grandpa are a study in opposites—just like Mom and Dad. Grandfather doesn't have any prison tattoos. In fact, the closest he's ever been to jail is the time he went to bail out my dad when he was married to Mom—and that's a long story. Grandfather's very tall, with elegant white hair—and he likes to remind me that he still has all his teeth. In the pages of the society columns, he's what they call a good catch. In fact, ever since my grandmother passed away ten years ago, all the rich older ladies in New York City have been hoping to snag him. Actually, even women my mom's age flirt with him. He occasionally takes someone to a ball or event, but Grandmother was his love, so more often than not, I am his "date."

In the limo Mom's cell phone rang. She answered it. "Hello, David. Yes, she's right here." She handed the phone to me, and it was the mayor telling me what a wonderful time he had on our excursion.

"Thanks," I said. "I had a nice time, too."

"I'm not giving up, Lulu. We're going to do that

again until I win you over, just like I won over your mother."

Okay, so this was my first clue my luck was turning. I mean, I had a nice time, but I didn't need to do it again.

"Great," I said, with as much fake enthusiasm as I could muster. I handed the phone back to Mom. She chatted for a minute, then closed her phone.

"Is he going to be there?" I asked her.

"Later. He has to speak at a dinner for the dedication of the statue honoring the fallen NYPD during Nine-eleven."

I nodded. Then her cell phone rang again. She answered it and again handed it to me. I couldn't imagine what else the mayor had to say—only it wasn't the mayor. It was Dad. And he was angry.

"I thought I told you to stay away from Mark."

I shook my head. From bad to worse. "You didn't say absolutely, positively. You made a suggestion. But I can make my own decisions."

"Look, a boy like that can only be trouble."

I thought of the rich guys I'd played poker with. They were cutthroat and spoiled. Mark was neither of those things.

"You don't know him, Dad."

"I know he's never going to amount to anything. He's bad news. In fact, he reminds me of me when I was that age."

"You're not bad news," I said.

"Lulu, you'll end up with a gambler like me over my dead body."

I wanted to tell him that it was his fault I gambled and liked Vegas and boxing and football. But I knew better than to argue with him when he was in a bad mood. "I'm on my way to Grandfather's. Dad, you're just going to have to trust me. You always used to."

Dad was quiet for a moment. It was true. He and I had the best relationship of any of my friends and their dads. I mean, Dack's father always had a reason why it was inconvenient for Dack to spend his weekends with him. Baywatch always had plans. Plus, Dack's mom said his father was trying to get Baywatch accepted in his social circle, so they were constantly attending various events. But Baywatch was so dumb, she couldn't hold a conversation to save her life, so they were, according to Dack's mom, in "social Siberia."

"All right, Lulu. I'm trusting you. For now."

"Love you."

"Love you, too."

I handed the cell phone back to Mom and rolled my eyes after she closed it. "I see the two of you are tag-teaming me."

"It's not like that."

"Isn't it?"

"Lulu . . . all we want is for you to have the kind of future you deserve."

"Mom, stop worrying. It's not every guy—uptown or downtown—who'll spend an entire day at a museum with you just because you like it. I'm sure he would have much rather done something else. But he went because he likes me, and he was trying to learn more about art."

My mother smiled and laughed a little.

"What?"

"Oh, nothing." She waved her hand. "I was just remembering a time when I took your father to a black-tie affair. I could tell he despised it. Just hated every moment of all those puffed-up penguins in tuxes. But he went. And he tried to fit in. And then they came out with finger bowls. Sliced lemons and violet flowers floated in them. Sterling silver bowls. And your father started to eat it like soup."

I couldn't help laughing. "No way!"

"Oh, yes," she said, smiling at the memory. "And

your grandfather had no idea what to make of him. But I thought it was rather sweet that he was making the effort."

We arrived at Grandfather's town house. He owns two of them, actually, prewar buildings that he combined into one huge residence. He knocked down a bunch of interior walls to make a small ballroom, where tonight there would be dinner and dancing. Tonight's shindig was for a mentoring program he sponsored.

I walked into the party, and Grandfather spotted me. "Now, there's the girl of my heart." He beamed. I walked over to him and he gave me a kiss on my cheek. "You look flushed. Are you feeling okay?"

I exchanged glances with Mom. "I feel fine. I just had to rush a bit to get ready."

"Well, you look lovely, so save a dance for me. But in the *meantime*, the son of Harold Davis Walker is here. The oil baron. He'd be a nice catch."

"I'm not fishing, Grandfather."

"Oh, you say that now, but wait until you meet him."

I sighed as Grandfather steered me to the buffet line and introduced me to Harold Davis Walker III—

who, I was thankful, went by Dave and not Harold. He was gorgeous: blue eyes, blond hair, toothpaste-commercial smile. Perfectly pressed tuxedo with diamond cuff links. Slight tan. And he seemed nice enough. But it didn't matter to me. Mark was the guy I was crazy about.

"Care to dance?" Dave asked me.

"Sure." I shrugged.

On the parquet floor we slow-danced to "Unforgettable"—the Natalie Cole version.

"So, is your grandfather as serious about hooking you up with a Social Register brat as mine is?"

I laughed. "Exactly."

"I've heard about you."

"Oh?" I said suspiciously.

He leaned in close to my ear. "You have a wild streak. I hear you're a heck of a poker player."

"Who'd you hear that from?"

"I can't reveal my sources," he said, winking at me.

He stepped back and twirled me around. "I have a wild streak too. I like to sometimes ride my bike and not hold on to the handlebars." His voice was totally flirtatious.

"Oooh," I joked back. "Dangerous."

We danced and flirted some more. Then the song stopped playing. "Can I call you sometime, Miss Wild Child?"

"I kind of have a boyfriend."

"Just as friends. Come on; it'll make our grandfathers happy."

"Sure."

He escorted me back to my grandfather. "Thank you for letting me steal her away for a dance."

"Anytime, young man."

Grandfather took my arm and we walked toward some other partygoers.

"Grandfather?"

"Hmm?"

"You know this isn't the eighteen hundreds, right? There's no such thing as an arranged marriage anymore."

"I know. But there's nothing wrong with a good match." He patted my arm.

"Can I ask you something?"

"Certainly, Tallulah."

"What did you think when Mom ran off with Dad?"

"Oh . . . well, she was always a little headstrong.

And in the end, you just want your children to be happy. And we did get you out of the bargain." He gave me a squeeze.

I smiled at him. Hopefully my parents felt the same. Over the next couple of hours I danced and ate and tried to have a good time, all the while wishing Mark were there. Dave was a perfectly fine guy. But in the end, it's about sparks. And I had them with Mark.

I was looking forward to going home at the end of the night. The mayor arrived—which, of course, caused a stir. He was a very popular mayor. Crime was at an all-time low and job creation was high. Mom was all ... well, being Mom around the mayor, which meant she looked like she was a ten-year-old with a crush on her fifth-grade teacher. Dad may have been her "grand passion," as she put it, but I thought the mayor was starting to make her feel head over heels.

"Mom?" I asked her as she and the mayor started toward the dance floor yet again. "Could I take the limo back and you get a ride from David's limo?"

She looked at him and he, of course, nodded.

"Sure, darling. Off you go."

"Great!" I wanted to call Mark. I wanted out of my heels and my fancy dress. I wanted to scrub off my makeup and let down my hair.

I kissed my grandfather good-bye and headed out to the car. When I got there, I pulled my cell phone out of my purse. I'd had it off the whole night, since I wouldn't have been able to hear it over the music anyway. The first thing I did was check for messages from Mark. There was one, a text message:

HAD A GR8T TIME.
CALL ME 2MORROW.
LV MARK.

Then I had, oddly, five text messages from Dack. All with "911" on them. Urgent. I called my voice mail and the same thing: "Lulu, please, please, please call me. Right away. The *second* you get this."

As the driver pulled away from the curb, I called Dack's cell.

"Dack?"

"Oh, man, thank God you called."

"What? What's going on?"

"Something really bad, Lulu."

My mind raced. "Is something wrong with your mom? Your dad?" I swallowed. "Baywatch?" I imagined her breast implants getting punctured and deflating like a life raft with a leak.

"No."

"Please don't tell me you gambled again."

"Oh, no way. Believe me. Never again. I'm cured."

"What then?" I felt frantic.

"Are you sitting down?"

"I'm in a friggin' limo. Yeah."

"Lulu, when you get home, when you're *alone,* open your e-mail. Lulu . . . you're being blackmailed."

Chapter Ten

Lulu's Rule of Poker #10:
Sometimes the other guy has all the cards.

I had no idea what Dack was talking about, but he told me it would be better if I waited until I got home. As soon as the limo pulled up to my building, I said good night to the driver and bolted up to my apartment.

I unlocked the door, locked it again behind me, dropped my velvet wrap and my purse, and raced to my room. I booted up my computer, willing it to start faster, and checked my e-mails. And there it was. From an address I didn't know. Nickname? Pokerfiend.

I opened it. No message, but a JPEG file clip.

I clicked on it, and the movie clip launched. I sat down in my desk chair, stunned, and started trembling.

It was me. Dealing cards. Talking about how I had learned poker hands before my multiplication tables. Me earning big pots. Me earning the watch back. Me talking about all the illegal poker games I'd been to with my dad. This was so not good.

I called Dack. "What is going on? What is this? I was taped?"

"I see you got the clip."

"Yeah. This isn't good. I have no idea what they're up to. I mean . . . if they're going to go to the police with it, they're just as guilty."

"Close out of that and open the second one. The subject line is 'Invitation.'"

I closed the film, which was making me queasy looking at it anyway. I scanned my in-box. Spam and e-mails from Angie—she loves to send me links to fan sites for our favorite movie stars— filled most of it. Then I spotted it. From Poker-fiend again.

Dear Lulu:

   Meet me at the Starbucks on Fifty-
fourth and Lex. Five o'clock tomorrow.
Don't think you want to be late.

   The Fiend

Okay, so now I was rapidly turning from nervous and scared to angry.

"What the heck is this, Dack?"

"I'm not sure, but you're not going to that meeting alone."

"It's not like they're going to do anything to me out in public."

"Just the same, I'm going."

I played the clip again and had a very uneasy feeling. Maybe it had been too easy winning the watch back. Maybe everyone—the weird older guy, the college student, Chip, Carter—was involved in a setup of some kind. But how? And more important, why?

I was totally freaked out. I mean, my dad wouldn't care. He would care that I lied to my mother about where I was, but he wouldn't care beyond that. In my dad's world, playing illegal cards isn't a big deal. *Cheating* at illegal cards would be a bigger deal to him. It's the principle of the thing when you sit down at the poker table. Mom, on the other hand, would be upset. She doesn't like my card-playing hobby to begin with. But someone didn't make this file to get me in trouble with my mother. Would the police care? Was it a misdemeanor?

I unzipped my dress with my phone resting on my shoulder. "I don't like this, Dack."

"Well, we'll see what this guy wants tomorrow."

"And who's the fiend? Chip? Carter?"

"I don't know."

"All right, listen ... I'll see you tomorrow at Starbucks."

That night I tried to sleep, but I kept having visions of cards attacking me, like in *Alice in Wonderland*. I couldn't sleep, and worse, I wanted to lie there and think about Mark and replay our whole date in my head, but instead I was cringing at everything I had said on the hidden camera. From looking at it, I figured it was a security camera from the apartment. Rich people have security cameras and nanny-cams.

The next day I met Dack at 4:30 a block from the Starbucks, and we walked in together. We looked around at the small round tables and the line of people waiting for their coffee drinks, scanning for a familiar face. Then we spotted him—the old guy. Well, not old, but the thirty-something man from the poker game—Al. He was standing in line.

I walked over to him, Dack just a step behind me. "Okay, Al—if that's even your real name—what do you want?"

"Can I get you a latte?" he said casually, knowing he would infuriate me.

"No," I snapped. "You can tell me what you want."

Just then a barista called out, and he collected his coffee drink. "Follow me." He motioned, and we went to a table at the back.

I plopped into a chair and folded my arms. Dack just glared at him.

"It's simple, really." He smiled, only it was a cold and nasty smile. "I represent a consortium of investors."

"Investors," I said incredulously.

"Yes. And we've been looking for a phenom."

"A what?" Dack asked.

"A phenom," he said dryly. "A poker-playing phenom. Someone we can back in some very exclusive games. Highly illegal, of course. And very high stakes."

"Unbutton your shirt," I ordered him, while I looked around. I wasn't about to be taped again. No one else looked interested in our conversation, though.

"Why?" he asked.

"I want to make sure you're not wearing a wire. And while you're at it, empty your pockets."

He looked irritated. He lifted his shirt up, rather than unbutton it. A flabby stomach, but no wire. Then he emptied his pockets. Nothing but a wallet, keys, and a tin of Altoids.

"So why me?" I asked.

"We heard through some associates that you were an amazingly good player, impossible to read. A true poker face, to use the cliché. And we got to thinking, if we backed you in the game, you would be highly underestimated by the other players, which would, of course, allow you to make the proverbial killing."

My head was pounding near my temple. Who *was* this guy?

"So why the file clip?" I asked, narrowing my eyes.

"We didn't think you'd do it otherwise. You don't need the money. And you apparently play more for the fun than anything else."

"What if I'm not interested?"

"Then the file clip goes to the media."

Dack snorted. "Like she cares."

But my face, I knew, had turned pale.

Al leaned back in his chair and calmly sipped his coffee. "I knew it would hit you, kiddo. She'll do it. I don't think the mayor's girlfriend's daughter needs to be splashed all over the evening news—especially since he's due to announce whether or not he's going to run again."

I don't have a poker face for nothing, though. I bluffed. "I don't even *like* the mayor. So I don't particularly care whether he and my mother stay together or break up."

"Sure. That's why you went out for a little bonding time on Wednesday."

Was I being followed? Now I was really mad—and worried. I didn't like this game at all.

"So she'll tell her father, and you don't want to mess with him," Dack countered. Which was true. My dad was *not* someone whose bad side you wanted to be on.

"I don't think so. The way he'll handle it will be an even bigger mess in the media. She doesn't want her dad to know just so he *doesn't* get involved.

No . . . I think little Tallulah here will play ball. Or, rather, poker."

I stood up. "Who are you?"

"I told you. I represent a consortium."

Dack stood and gave me a look like, *Let's get out of here.*

"I'll think about it. But I wouldn't count on it. So I hope you're ready to mail your clip to the media, because in poker you either put up or shut up."

Al stared up at me calmly. "You want to play with the big boys, you'd better know who's got an ace in the hole."

"What the heck is that supposed to mean?" Dack asked.

"Never mind," I whispered.

"Twenty-four hours. Decide. Or the clip goes to Page Six of the *Post*."

I grabbed my purse and left the coffee shop with Dack following me.

"What did he mean, ace in the hole?" Dack asked.

I sighed. "You really are *so* much better off not playing poker. He means that I'd better not bluff. If I tell him to go to the media, he'll do it. And more. He's got an ace in the hole—that means he's hiding something else. A trump card. He knows poker. And he knows blackmail."

"So let him go to the media. Chip, Carter, they'll all be in trouble."

We walked up the block, a cold wind hitting our faces. "Dack, I don't think that matters."

"Of course it matters. They're not going to want to be part of this—their families would all freak out. They can't get away with this, Lulu."

When we got two blocks away I stopped and faced Dack.

"You don't get it."

"What?"

"I was set up. Chip, Carter . . . we all were. Somehow this guy infiltrated their little game. Look at how old he is. And check out what he wears. Very expensive stuff, Dack. He's not some punk. He's, like, thirty or something. And he obviously had a plan going into that game. This isn't about Chip and Carter and those stupid losers. This is about me, playing in a big-time game. I don't want to do it."

"So don't."

But I thought of my mother twirling on the dance floor with David, beaming. I thought of him blowing off the fancy dinner to take me for a hot dog and a walk in Central Park.

I had really gotten myself in a mess of epic proportions. Worst of all, I risked hurting my mother, who has always been there for me.

"I have to think about it, Dack. This time the stakes are really high."

Chapter Eleven

Lulu's Rule of Poker #11:
Just when you think the stakes
can't get higher . . . they will.

That night I was invited to a party at my friend
Chloe's apartment. I decided not to go, even
though her boyfriend is a deejay and she always has
the hottest music. I was in no mood to be around
people. Even Dack. He called and wanted to come
over to watch DVDs—his mom was recovering from
Botox and a chemical peel, and his dad and Baywatch
had jetted off to Jamaica for the weekend—but I told
him I didn't feel well.

Truthfully, I felt fine. Just sorry for myself. How had I let myself get into such a mess?

Around eleven Mark called. I was lying in bed watching TV and pressed mute.

"I've been thinking about you," he said when I answered. Even his voice gave me shivers.

"I've been thinking about you, too."

"And you won't believe it, but I've been thinking about Goya. How do you like that? You might teach me some book smarts after all. Me, knowing stuff about dead guys who paint. Not bad."

"You never know. You could become a curator someday."

"I'm barely squeaking through high school, but who knows . . . maybe someday I'll go to college."

"What would you study? Let me guess . . . art history?"

"No offense, Lulu. I liked the museum because you were with me. But come on . . . not very practical. No, I was thinking more along the lines of accounting. I'm really good with numbers. Always have been."

"Good for you."

"Are you mad at me?"

"Huh? No. Why?"

"You sound really ... distracted. Is everything okay, Lulu? You know, if anyone ever bothers you ... well, they'd be messing with the wrong girl." He gave a little laugh. "Just kidding. I know that sounds really cavemannish, but still. I would break the legs of anyone who hurt you. Come on, tell me. What's eating you?"

I rolled onto my side on the bed and looked out at the Manhattan skyline. That was the difference between my mom's world and Dad's world. If Dad or Mark knew about this guy Al, they *would* break his legs. Or at least do something drastic. And I didn't want either Dad or Mark getting into trouble with the law. My problem had to stay my problem only. I wanted to tell Mark, but I realized I couldn't.

"It's nothing."

"Is it your parents ... upset about us seeing each other?"

"No. I promise. It's not that."

"Next weekend you're at your father's, right?"

"Yeah."

"So will you go to your grandfather's bar on Friday?"

"Probably. It's kind of our routine."

"Then I'll see you there. I miss ya, Lulu."

"Miss you, too."

"And I'll win over your father. Believe me. I will. So listen, good night. Hope Lady Luck is good to you, my poker girl."

"Thanks. But right about now, I think Lady Luck has left the building, as they say."

I closed my phone and pulled the covers up and over my head. I wanted to hide from the world.

About ten minutes later I heard my mother calling me.

"I'm in my room," I shouted.

Next thing I knew, Mom *and* the mayor came waltzing in.

"Wake up and have champagne with us," the mayor said.

"I am awake," I replied cautiously, peering out from the covers. I looked at my mother, who was positively glowing. Forget butterflies in my stomach; it felt like bats were swarming in there. Part of me wanted to freeze time, so I wouldn't have to hear what I knew was coming next.

"David asked me to marry him," my mother gushed, and thrust out her hand.

"Holy cow!" I said, sitting bolt upright. Her engagement ring was a Tiffany diamond the size of a large marble. "Wow!" I tried to sound excited. "I'm really happy for you guys."

"Come on!" David stuck his hand out toward me. "Out of bed. I have a surprise for you, too."

Just what I needed. More surprises.

I climbed out of bed, wearing my sloppy old sweats and a big T-shirt, and followed David and Mom into the living room.

Mom held her hand out in the light. "Isn't the ring beautiful, Lulu?"

"It is, Mom." I was happy for her. I really was. And unlike her and my dad, she and David were a good match. They fit like two pieces of a puzzle.

They had a bottle of Kristal champagne, and David popped the cork. Mom got three champagne flutes from the china cabinet, and David poured us each a glass, the bubbles fizzing in the golden-amber liquid.

"To the two most beautiful girls in Manhattan," he toasted. "My future wife and stepdaughter. You've made me the happiest man in New York."

He was eloquent and elegant off the cuff. He had a lot of practice as the mayor. Then he totally surprised me.

"Lulu . . . this is for you." He pulled a small powder blue Tiffany box from his pocket.

I looked at him, totally confused.

"Open it." He smiled at me.

I had never gotten anything from Tiffany before. I'm not into jewelry, but if I were, well, those little blue boxes are the way to go. I put down my champagne glass, undid the little white bow, then lifted the lid off. Inside was a velvet box. I took it out, opened it, and gasped. It was a beautiful platinum cocktail ring with several small diamonds in a modern setting.

"Do you like it?"

"It's beautiful," I whispered.

"Lulu," he said, "I know you didn't ask for your mom to get into some high-profile romance. And I know you don't want to live in Gracie Mansion, or live in a fishbowl, but sometimes families have to try things. And I will try my hardest to make us a real family so that all that high-profile stuff doesn't matter. Okay?"

I nodded, feeling a little choked up. He was being so nice. I had so many friends with nightmare step-monsters. I really was lucky, I knew.

"Try it on. But read the inscription first," he said, looking pretty pleased with himself.

I lifted the ring from its box. Inside the band it read:

To Lulu, My New York Girl. Love, David

I slipped it on my right ring finger, and it fit perfectly. It sparkled. "Thank you."

"Come on, drink your champagne," the mayor said. "What a night!"

He and Mom sat down on the couch and snuggled, and the three of us talked.

"Now," Mom said. "We don't want to tell anyone yet. We're telling Grandfather, and your dad, of course. But we're not announcing it to the media yet. We want the three of us to enjoy it just for a few days, you know? Without all the intrusions."

Like the intrusions that would come if that file clip was now leaked to the media? I gulped and nodded.

"And I know it's your mother's second marriage, but it's my first ... and heck, I want it to be a big wedding. And we want you to help us plan every detail."

"Great."

"We have flowers to pick, dresses," Mom said. "Linens and menus, and a cake."

"Buttercream frosting," said David. "My favorite."

"A million little details to plan," Mom said, smiling.

Somehow I didn't imagine that included Mom tossing the bouquet to a rabid press corps wanting to rip the mayor to shreds for having a stepdaughter who gambled illegally.

As I looked at the very beautiful diamond ring as it caught the light and gave off a rainbow of colors, I realized that I was going to have to do it. I was going to have to gamble for the creep named Pokerfiend.

Chapter Twelve

Lulu's Rule of Poker #12:
Know when to fold.

Yeah, yeah, yeah. The Kenny Rogers song. You
have to know when to hold 'em and know when
to fold 'em. I get it. And I knew that, at least for the
moment, Pokerfiend had all the cards. It was time to
fold. To give in.

However, I didn't want to seem overanxious
either. I didn't reply to his e-mails until exactly
twenty-four hours later. Then I got an e-mail from
him. Subject line?

Are you ready to run with the big dogs?

Well, I was ready to bite like a pit bull, but for now, yeah. I clicked reply and wrote back:

```
Dear Fiend:

    You win. Send me details—where, when,
etc.

    Lulu
```

I called Angie while I was on the computer and told her about the whole thing. She said, "What if you lose on purpose? Just lose all their money. That'll teach that jerk."

"Somehow I don't see these guys being happy about that. Look at all the trouble they went to in the first place to film me and everything."

"Very creepy."

"I know."

"So you're really going to go live in Gracie Mansion?"

"Yeah. You can't tell anyone, though."

"My lips are sealed. Man ... I feel so sorry for you. It's not like you can break curfew when you have a bunch of bodyguards."

"I know. It really, really sucks."

"Does your dad know about this poker dude?"

"No. You know how he is."

"Yup. Very gangsta."

"Exactly. Besides, I got myself into this mess. I'll get myself out of it. I hope."

Suddenly my computer dinged.

"I've got e-mail. Gotta run, Angie."

It was from the Fiend.

```
Game is on. Suite 1487, Grand Hyatt.
Seven p.m. sharp. Friday. Come alone.
```

Friday was my Dad weekend. It was my time to see Mark. I wrote back:

```
Friday night is no good.
```

Fiend wrote back. Quickly.

```
$100,000 on the line. Too bad if it's
no good.
```

And he attached the movie clip again. I hated him! I typed an e-mail back.

```
Fine. And what assurance do I have
that this is it? This one game?
```

I waited.

```
   None. But if we win, we'll be satis-
fied.
```

Great. And what if they lost?

On Wednesday, Dad and I had dinner together. He took me to our place in Little Italy. It's actually a total pain to get to, but the food is amazing. I ordered ravioli that they make fresh every day and hand-stuff—this night they were filled with ricotta and mushrooms. Dad got his usual—spaghetti Bolognese. He never tries anything new. That's why he says he'll never remarry. "Can't teach an old dog new tricks," is his motto.

"Dad?" I asked him while we ate our garlic bread.

"Hmm?"

"Um, Mom was working late tonight."

"Yeah?"

"Well, she wanted to talk to you. About something. And she was really upset she couldn't be there when you came to get me."

"What? You're not in trouble, are you?"

"No." I didn't know how to say it, so I just blurted it out. "She's getting married."

My father stopped midbite and didn't move for a

full thirty seconds. Then he blinked slowly a couple of times. "Married?"

"Yeah. To the mayor. Though I guess you probably figured that part out."

He didn't say anything for a minute. Then he sipped his red wine and said, "Well, good for her."

"You're not upset?"

"No. I mean, Lulu . . ." He rolled up his shirt-sleeve to where it said ELLIE and LULU with a heart on his bicep in blue-black ink. "I loved that woman as much as any man can love a woman. But I can't live with her."

I was relieved. I didn't want to picture my father sad that my mom had moved on. Even if it was, after all, fifteen years later.

"How do you feel about it, Lulu?"

I crunched into some garlic bread, chewed, and swallowed. "I don't want to live in Gracie Mansion; that's for sure. But as stepfathers go, he's a nice one. He's gone out of his way to get to know me."

"I guess I'm going to have to meet this guy sooner or later."

"Probably." I sipped my Coke.

"I didn't vote for him."

I burst out laughing. "Oh, be sure to tell him that."

The two of us grinned. Then I had to lie. "Oh . . . I almost forgot, Dad. I have to go with Dack to the school play on Friday. He's the assistant director, and then there's an after-party. I promised him ages ago before I knew it was your weekend. Can I just come over Saturday to Sunday?"

"Sure. Tell Dack I said hi. Now *that's* the kind of guy you should be dating. Not some tattooed tough guy."

"Hello? Pot? The black kettle is calling."

He rolled down the sleeve where his tattoos were.

"Dad?"

"Yeah?"

"Do you think I'm ready to play in a big-time poker tournament?"

"High stakes?"

I nodded.

"Lulu, you were born ready. You've been playing since you could hold cards in your hand. Of course, you know Grandpa wants you to go to the World Series of Poker. I think you'd do fine. But you're not old enough."

"Well, for a legitimate tournament. But what about an illegal one?"

"You know, those are trouble. Sometimes you have some really nasty characters. The mob. Listen, you keep playing at the bar. A few hundred. You're getting lots of experience, and someday, if you really want to, Grandpa and I will back you in a legitimate tournament. Promise."

"But do you think I'm ready?"

Dad stared at me.

"What?" I asked.

"Do you see a turnip truck parked outside on the streets of Little Italy?"

"Huh?"

"Do I look like I fell off the turnip truck? Like I was born yesterday? This isn't a hypothetical question, is it?"

"No." I had to think fast. "I was *offered* a chance to play in a tournament, Dad. But I didn't take it. I just was wondering."

He looked at me skeptically, but in the end said, "All right. But I mean it. Keep clear of trouble."

I nodded, feeling guilty, but I just couldn't tell him the whole story. And what I hoped was that I'd win and never have to.

The two of us finished dinner.

When I got home, I phoned Mark with the bad

news that I wasn't going to be going to my dad's until Saturday.

"Lulu . . . I have to see you Friday. Come on." His voice was sexy. "You have more stuff to teach me."

I could think of a few things he could teach me. But I didn't say anything.

"How about if I come to Dack's play, too? Then I'll take you to this party and then out for something to eat."

"No!" I said a little too hastily.

"What?" He paused. "I get it . . . I'm not good enough for your rich friends?"

"That's not it at all."

"Yeah, it is. I'm fine for when you're at your father's, but you sure don't want me around the trust-fund guys you hang out with."

"Mark . . ."

"Then tell me why you don't want me to come to the play. I mean, I don't even want to see a stupid play. I'd be doing it to spend time with you."

"I . . . Mark, listen, it's just that . . ." I struggled for something to say, but no words came out.

"Believe me, Lulu. I get it." And at that, Mark hung up on me.

I folded my cell phone and felt like I was going to cry. How had everything gotten so screwed up? I needed to play in that poker game—and win—and be through with these creeps once and for all so I could go back to my so-called normal life.

Chapter Thirteen

Lulu's Rule of Poker #13:
Know how to bluff.

On Friday night I told my mom the same phony story as my dad about the school play. I was smart enough to choose something that was actually sort of true: A school play was, indeed, going on at Baxter. The hopelessly bitchy Tiffany Carrington was the lead. But Dack wasn't the assistant director. His clubs ranged from the debate society (his father nagged him for a future career as a lawyer—no matter that Dack didn't want to be a lawyer) to Amnesty International.

I didn't want to go to the game alone, but I knew I couldn't walk in there with Dack. Still, I was raised with my dad's buddies. I wasn't stupid enough to walk into *any* hotel room alone. So Dack and I had a plan.

On Friday I dressed down. The idea wasn't to play up my sexiness, like in our silly strip poker games with Dack. The idea was to get the other players to think I was a kid—a real kid, who stood no chance against grizzled pros.

I donned a pair of jeans with rips at the knees, and opted for a pair of sneakers. I didn't wear any makeup at all, and I pulled my hair into a high pony-tail. I wanted to look as young as possible. If I could have given myself acne I would have!

For a shirt, I outdid myself. I found a Hello Kitty one with rhinestones. Pretty in pink. That was what I was aiming for. But the real stroke of total genius?

I put in my old retainer!

Dack came over at six and howled at my outfit. "You look like you did in sixth grade—except with a slightly bigger chest."

"Thanks." I shot him a dirty look.

"Okay, now, here we go." Dack had an array of gadgets, which he laid out on my bed.

"If they think I'm wired, they'll be really pissed," I said.

"I know. All we want is for you to be *safe,* so that if I hear anything crazy going on, I call your dad." I decided my dad was better than the police. Though if Dad realized I totally lied to his face, well, maybe the police would be a better choice.

He stuck a tiny little round bugging device on the inside of my shirt.

"Your mother really used this stuff?"

"Yup. As soon as she suspected Baywatch really couldn't type—which she can't—she guessed she wasn't a secretary. She bugged my dad's office, his coat, his car. Why do you think she got such a good settlement?"

I shook my head in amusement.

"I'll be listening through this." He showed me a small transistor-like device. "I'll be in the room three doors down—I told the hotel manager I was superstitious and had stayed there last time."

Whereas I was trying to look younger, Dack had on a suit, so he looked like a young executive on a business trip. He had a briefcase and everything. He looked cute, and being six feet tall helped.

"Okay. We ready to do this?"

"Yeah."

We left my apartment and took a cab to the hotel. I went up separately while Dack checked in. I knocked on the door. Pokerfiend answered. I could see the suite was being set up for a major game. There were three separate tables, three dealers, and waitresses and a bartender.

"If it isn't the kid." He smiled at me. "Come on in. I'd offer you a drink, but that would be illegal. Glass of milk?"

I glared at him. "No, thanks."

Several of my opponents were seated on couches, and they looked me over. Unlike in my dad's games, which usually had a motley assortment of ex-cons, tough guys, and old-timers, the other players were sharply dressed, and most of them were wearing expensive sunglasses, so I couldn't see their eyes.

I got it in an instant.

I wasn't going to be playing typical illegal poker players. I was going to be playing against stockbrokers and investment bankers and hot young movers and shakers in the finance and corporate worlds who played poker to unwind. They'd watched too much *Celebrity Poker Showdown* and thought they were real poker players. They bet for the thrill—but more than that, guys like this bet for their egos. Michael Jordan, the king of basketball, used to bet big money on his golf game. He had all the money in the world. Why let a million bucks or whatever ride on a par-three hole on a golf course? Because a part of him was an adrenaline junkie, and off the court that was hard to reproduce, I guess.

These guys likely worked ninety hours a week. My dad calls them the young turks of Wall Street. My guess is their hobbies were beautiful women and the hottest clubs in Manhattan, but most of them were too busy to devote time to any true extreme sport, like mountain climbing. They didn't have the time to train, to take trips to far-off places. No . . . this was easy. They could sit in a hotel suite until four in the morning for bragging rights.

I smiled. It still would come down to the cards and to my smarts at the table, but now I knew. I knew who "they" were. The other players didn't scare me. I knew what I would be up against. They, on the other hand, knew nothing about me.

And that was good.

I also knew that guys like that wouldn't back down. And that would be their downfall. Being shown up by a teenager in a Hello Kitty shirt would make them nuts. It would be emasculating. So they would bet high and bet foolishly. They would play aggressively until they made a fatal mistake at the table.

"There's a buffet over there." Fiend pointed it out. Sushi, smoked salmon, and other high-end appetizers filled a table.

"Not hungry," I said.

"All right. Let's get started."

Their game was Hold 'Em, and from what I understood, these guys all had to front some major money even to sit at the table—all of which went into Fiend's pocket. What they didn't know, of course, was that Fiend wasn't content with just a cut from the table. He wanted it all. So he was backing me. That would be like the casinos in Vegas putting professional players on the tables to hedge their bets. This guy was slick. He was putting a ringer at the table—and blackmailing me on top of it.

I smiled my biggest smile, showing off my shiny metal retainer. "Well, boys," I said, a sight lisp to my S from wearing my unfamiliar retainer, "are we ready to cut the cards?"

Because I was ready.

Ready to play and then be finished with this entire fiasco.

Chapter Fourteen

Lulu's Rule of Poker #14:
Sometimes poker is about psyching out your opponents.

Three tables of Hold 'Em were going on at the same time. Eventually the five best players would sit together at one table for the finals. At my table were four guys who definitely thought they were right out of *Ocean's Eleven*. One by one they fell.

Beaten by a girl with a ponytail and a Hello Kitty shirt.

When one of them stood up, he leaned over really close to me and whispered, "I can't wait to watch Matt mop up the table with you."

I guessed Matt was their best player.

But Matt had never played me.

The evening wore on. Finally it was down to me and three guys—Matt included.

Matt turned out to be a guy with a seat on the New York Stock Exchange.

"Youngest guy to earn a seat," he said proudly, and he blew a big puff of cigar smoke at my face.

"Wow," I said. "A seat on the New York Jerk Exchange. And you think that makes you a good poker player?" I raised one eyebrow.

"Isn't it your bedtime, little girl?" he asked me.

I looked at my watch. "Nah. I usually wait until I've beaten all the pretty boys who think they can play poker against me. It won't be long."

I could see the rage building. He was clenching his jaw, and his face was flushed. I would have been loving the moment if I weren't so resentful that I had to be there in the first place.

"Who decided to let some kid play with us, anyway?" he snarled.

"Seems the kid is beating the pants off you, gentlemen," Fiend piped up.

"Well," Matt said, rubbing his hands together, "time to teach her a little lesson about respect for her elders."

"Hmm," I said, batting my eyes. "My daddy always taught me to respect my elders ... *if* they're smarter than I am. But the dumb ones ... well, they get beat every time."

I wanted him good and mad! And I could see I was succeeding. At the same time, I was avoiding any eye contact with Fiend. If these guys thought for a second they were being set up, I was scared to see what they would do. I mean, it's not like a bunch of suits from Wall Street scare me, but I knew I was playing a dangerous game by getting these guys so angry. I was glad Dack was two rooms away with my father on speed dial if need be.

"Enough of your mouth, kid. Let's see what you're made of."

"Bring it on." I smiled.

My plan was working.

Chapter Fifteen

Lulu's Rule of Poker #15:
It helps to have an ace in the hole.

I was *this* close to winning. Matt was a good player. At least, I think he was. He beat his previous table. But against me . . . well, something about Hello Kitty and my retainer irritated him and messed with his judgment. He bet big every hand—even when the flop was lousy.

The chips in front of me grew. When I was a little girl I used to line them all up by color and stack them neatly, like a little city. Instead of LEGOs, I played with poker chips. But now I liked sweeping them over to me, spread out on the table in a mess. I liked hearing them clink together and felt like a character in a movie winning big, big, big and wanting to let it ride. The other players, who had hung around to drink, and who at first seemed to despise me, now stood around the table and smiled when I won. They also egged on Matt more, mocking him for losing to me—which only fit with my plan perfectly. The angrier he got, the worse he played.

We were down to what I guessed was going to be our last hand. And I had an ace in the hole. More precisely? I had two.

Now, having two aces was just luck, pure and simple. I'm a good player, but in this particular case I could have been the worst player in the room and still won. In my mind, I thanked Lady Luck and my dad's favorite, Saint Jude—the patron saint of hopeless causes. Dad's been known to silently pray to Saint Jude when the other guy's got a possible straight and Dad's got just two pair.

And so I knew I won. I did. Two aces! Matt bet it "all in"—all his chips. And I saw his bet. Just as I was about to say, "All right, show me your cards . . . ," the police barged in.

"Freeze! Everyone stay where you are."

Two guys in blazers were holding up shields. "NYPD. Please stay exactly as you are."

I wanted to jump out the window. If I thought Fiend's little file clip might mess things up for Mom and the mayor, what, pray tell, would an *arrest* do?

Matt and the other guys were sputtering something about it being a friendly game. Two guys were already dialing their lawyers. Four more cops streamed into the room.

Fiend looked at me. "You set me up, didn't you?"

I shook my head. "You have no idea how much I so do not want to be dealing with the police right now."

The police were going to each guy and putting him in plastic handcuffs—the cuffs looked like twist ties from plastic garbage bags.

"We'll be getting your statements," said one officer, a dark-haired guy with intense black eyes. He looked around, and it was like all of a sudden he spotted me—retainer and all.

I watched as he took in the megapile of chips in front of me. I obviously wasn't going to be able to get away with saying I didn't know the first thing about gambling. Poker? What poker game?

My heart was pounding, and my hands were shaking. I had never been in so much trouble in my life. This was like breaking curfew and flunking math all in one fell swoop. Worse. Next I heard a knock on the door.

"Excuse me? Is my client here? Miss Tallulah King? There you are, Tallulah."

My mouth dropped open. There stood Dack pretending he was a lawyer. He had a suit on, but unless he started law school in sixth grade, no one would believe he was really an attorney. *Maybe* a stockbroker's intern. But an *attorney*. All I could think was, *Dack, Dack . . . what are you doing?!*

"And you are?" the cop asked, kind of amused.

"Dalton Kensington the Third, Esquire."

I had to give Dack credit: All those years of debate club meant he could talk a good game, and his voice was confident without a hint of nervousness. But face it: He had to shave maybe once a month at best, and I could see he had a zit on his forehead. Lawyer? Yeah, right.

"Are you, now? And do you have some sort of identification, Mr. Kensington?"

Dack patted at his suit jacket, pretending to look for his ID. "Funny thing . . . I seem to have left my wallet in my other suit."

With one smooth motion the cop spun Dack

around and pulled his wallet from his back pants pocket. "Did you now, Dalton? Student at Baxter, I see. Dalton Kensington the Third. Well, at least you didn't lie about your name. Baxter? Isn't that where all the super-rich brats go? Let me guess. Your dad is the software king."

Dack nodded slowly. After all, he was named after his father.

"Okay . . . you two are coming with us."

"Do we have to?" I managed to squeak.

"Well, let me see, Miss . . . King, is it? You're sitting here, underage, playing poker with a bunch of guys—winning, I might add. And my guess is"—he eyeballed the chips—"no one planned on telling the IRS about their winnings. Never mind that gambling is illegal."

"Crap."

Dack and I were led away as still more officers arrived at the hotel room to arrest the other players. In the elevator on the way down to the lobby, Dack leaned over to me and whispered, "My mother's going to kill me."

I looked over at him and then down at the diamond ring on my right hand.

"I think by the time this is all over, Dack, I'm going to wish I were dead."

Chapter Sixteen

Lulu's Rule of Poker #16:
If arrested, use your lone call to phone Dad, not Mom.

At the station, all I knew to do was what every ex-con my father hung out with—including my grandfather—told me to do: I exercised my right to remain silent.

Dack, on the contrary, blabbed to everyone. He tried explaining the whole thing with the Fiend and the original poker game and the lost watch, and it seemed like he kept digging a bigger and bigger hole for himself. For us both.

Eventually they let Dack make his phone call. He

called his mom, who went shrieking for her bottle of Xanax before she even got in her limo to retrieve him. She arrived with the family attorney, a guy in an expensive suit even at that late hour of one in the morning. He was screaming about rights and questioning juveniles without their parents present. The three of them left, Dack's mom shrieking, before my father got to the station house. He was very calm. He talked to the police. Then he collected me, and we got in a cab and headed for his house.

He didn't say anything, and I was too afraid to. He sat next to me in the cab, staring straight ahead, clenching and unclenching his jaw. I was so unused to him being angry with me, I started crying—not out loud, but I couldn't help the tears splashing from my cheeks onto my Hello Kitty shirt. I sniffled once, and Dad looked my way.

"School play, huh?"

"I'm sorry I lied."

"I suspected as much. You're too headstrong for your own good, Lulu. Maybe your mother is right and we should send you to Paris, away from here. Learn how to be one of those snooty girls, not a cardplayer. Learn to be more like her and less like me."

My mother occasionally threatened boarding

school when I drank milk straight from the carton or left my room a mess, or when the hair spray and makeup on my bathroom counter got so sticky you needed a trowel to clean it. But she didn't mean it, and I knew he didn't. Not really.

"I don't see why I have to be one way or the other, Dad. Why can't I be like you *and* like her?"

"Because *she* doesn't get arrested."

I sniffled again. "Good point."

"I don't want you to lie to me anymore, Lulu."

"I won't. I promise. I am so, so, so sorry. I wish you could really *know* how sorry I am."

Dad nodded and looked out his window. Then he said softly, "I hear you were winning. In fact, I hear the cops peeked at the final hand. You had two aces in the hole. Good job, kiddo."

He patted me on the arm and then winked.

"That's it? That's all you're going to say?"

He nodded.

"You're not mad?"

"Nope. I mean, a little. About the lying."

I leaned back against the seat of the cab. "Have you called Mom yet?"

"Nope."

"She's going to be mad."

"Yup."

We rode through the night to his apartment. I got out of the cab and went inside, exhausted. "I kind of have to tell you the whole story, Dad." I didn't want him to think I would lie without a *really* good reason.

So I told him the whole thing, starting with the watch and ending with two aces in the hole.

"I understand, Lulu. But there's the matter of your—"

Before he could finish his sentence, his cell phone rang.

"Mother!" we both said together.

He answered, and I could hear her yelling—well, Mom doesn't yell so much as talk very forcefully—all the way over on the couch from where Dad was in his recliner. For his part, I heard a lot of "Yes, Ellie" and "No, Ellie," and then, thank goodness, "She's asleep." He was covering for me.

Eventually he closed his cell phone.

"Turn on channel two."

I lifted the remote and turned it on. "Oh, no," I said. Panic shot through me like bolts of electricity. There I was in living color, being led from the hotel.

The news anchor said, "As we told you, some breaking news tonight. First, the mayor of New York City announces his engagement to socialite and New York arts patron Eleanor King. And then, according to our sources at the police department, his future stepdaughter was involved in an illegal gambling operation. We've had no comment from the mayor's office yet, but we're *sure*"—the anchor's voice was very sarcastic—"he's going to have something to say."

The anchor's sidekick added, "Kids these days," as they again rolled the film.

You know, it's bad enough to mess up in private. But now all of New York City—from Staten Island to the Bronx to the Upper West Side—knew the trouble I was in.

Chapter Seventeen

Lulu's Rule of Poker #17:
Sometimes a wild card will come out of nowhere.

I hid at my father's all day on Saturday and refused to take my mother's calls. Dad kept talking to her, and I could tell she was getting angrier and angrier, but I just couldn't face her.

He hung up after yet another exchange and said, "Sooner or later, Lu, you're going to have to go home to her house, and you're going to have to deal with her. And the mayor."

I was lying on the couch, and I pulled a cushion over my head. "I'm staying here forever."

Dad clicked on the television with the remote.

"Argh!" I shouted.

The media was really going crazy with the story. Not just that I was clearly some juvenile delinquent, but the whole idea of "blended" families being a lot of work. Some TV shrinks were saying this was my way of crying out for help about my mother's remarriage. I mean, come on! This was about a watch. This was about helping Dack. This was about the Pokerfiend.

Dad switched to another channel. On *this* channel, the television shrink went through the signs of gambling addiction.

So now I was a gambling addict, diagnosed by someone who had never met me. I'd never been addicted to gambling in my life. I was the one who followed my own rules, and never bet what I couldn't afford to lose. I was always willing to walk away from a game. I loved to play, but it didn't rule my life.

And still, according to the media, the mayor had no comment. So that was it. I looked down at my ring. He hated me. He was probably going to break up with Mom. And forget about announcing his candidacy for reelection. I had ruined that. My heart sank. I couldn't imagine facing my mother. I pictured her dancing at Grandfather's, positively glowing. And then the night they came to my room to tell me about their engagement. I had ruined it.

It's bad enough to get into trouble on your own, but to get into trouble and hurt other people? I didn't think I could ever feel any worse.

"Dad, can we watch a DVD? These news breaks are driving me crazy."

"Sure thing, Lulu. What do you want to watch?"

"How about something funny to get my mind off things?"

"What about *Goodfellas*?"

"Great."

Now, maybe to some people that's not a funny movie, but Dad's from Hell's Kitchen, and he gets a kick out of how similar the movie is to his own experiences growing up in the neighborhood. It's like watching his friends on film. He thinks some of the one-liners are really funny, and Joe Pesci? Hysterical, because he's just like this guy Louie who Dad gambles with.

He put in the DVD, and I moped on the couch and watched it with him.

"Hungry?" Dad asked, pausing the movie about midway through.

"Not really."

"Lulu, I can have this guy taken care of. You know, break his legs or something. The one who filmed you."

"I know."

"And you could have told me."

"I know. I guess . . . I didn't want you getting in trouble, and I was embarrassed that I was in that much of a mess."

"Embarrassed?"

I nodded. "You've raised me to be street-smart. So I guess I just felt like I should be able to handle myself."

"Look, Lulu, even the most street-smart person in the world gets in over their head sometimes."

"You don't."

"You're kidding, right? Look, kiddo, I don't tell you all the stories of when I was your age because I don't want you to get any ideas. I want you to be like your mother. But trust me, I was in over my head a lot. And I guess as a father, I want to make sure you never make the same mistakes I did."

"I understand." My mother was the same way. Only for her, "trouble" meant not studying properly for her Latin final. It didn't mean juvenile delinquency.

"Next time, tell me. In the meantime you gotta eat something. Want some take-out Chinese?"

"All right," I said reluctantly. "My usual."

I loved that with my father, life was pretty ordinary. I had a "usual" from the local Chinese place. I could stay in my pj's all day. I didn't have to clean up after myself. We were slobs together.

Dad ordered our food—my usual is chicken with cashew nuts—and we resumed the movie. About twenty minutes later, there was a knock on the door.

"That was fast," Dad said. He paused the movie again and ran to get his wallet. My father doesn't believe in credit cards. Either that or with his rap sheet they won't give him one. He pulled out a wad of cash and crossed the room to the door. Like most New York apartments, it had a chain lock and a dead bolt. He undid both and opened it.

There, standing in the hallway of my father's apartment building, was the mayor of New York City.

Chapter Eighteen

Lulu's Rule of Poker #18:
The queen of hearts trumps all.

"I guess it's time we met." The mayor smiled at my dad and stuck out his hand.

"Jack King," my father said, his voice deep but friendly.

"David Walker."

"Come on in."

I sat up as the mayor, four bodyguards, and my mother walked into the apartment. My dad's place isn't that big. And there's not a lot of seating. Dad offered to bring in chairs from the kitchen, but apparently the bodyguards preferred to stand.

My mother came rushing over to me and kissed me on top of my head.

"That wasn't the reaction I was expecting, Mom." I was assuming I'd be grounded until I was old enough to collect social security.

"Dack came over with his mother. Once she calmed down . . . well, *calmed down* is a relative term. Calmed down, you know, for her. She was still a basket case, thinking this whole incident would keep him out of Harvard, but once she calmed down, she told me the whole thing. The watch, the film, the meeting at Starbucks."

I nodded. "So then you realize I am not a juvenile delinquent. Or a sociopath with a gambling problem."

Mom nodded. "You were trying to help Dack."

The mayor looked at my dad. "From what I understand, they won't be filing charges against her. It's more the media insanity that we have to deal with."

"It'll die down."

"Eventually, but now they're digging deeper into Ellie's background—which means they're gunning for you, too."

Dad sighed. "I suppose Ellie told you I've got a healthy rap sheet."

The mayor smiled wanly. "She mentioned it."

"We have ourselves a real mess."

"That we do."

Mom patted my hand. "You know, honey, if you had told us from the beginning, we could have helped you."

"It seemed too huge, Mom. And I didn't want to ruin your whole happy, I'm-getting-remarried vibe."

She nodded, and we were all quiet a moment. Then my cell phone vibrated. I had turned it to vibrate so I wouldn't have to hear it ring every few minutes with Mom calling, and I didn't want to deal with Dack or anyone. I had a text message. From Mark.

MEET ME ON THE CORNER. I'M WAITING.

Well, how was I supposed to pull that off?

"Dad, Mom? I need to get some fresh air."

My mother narrowed her eyes.

"I'm meeting Mark. He's at the corner. I'm sure he's worried about me."

My mother sighed.

"Come on, Mom. Look, I'm sure you, Dad, and David want to chat." I climbed off the couch. "Ten minutes. I swear."

Reluctantly, Mom nodded.

I pulled a scrunchie from my wrist and pulled my hair up in a ponytail. I knew I looked terrible, but there was no time to do anything else. I kissed my dad on the cheek as I left the apartment, cringing inside over what they might talk about while I was gone.

I raced down the stairs of Dad's building and burst out the front door. I could see Mark standing on the corner, and he waved. I ran over to him and threw my arms around his neck and gave him a hug.

"Lulu, man, I have been so worried about you."

"It's going to be okay. Sort of. I mean, I messed things up for the mayor."

He kissed my cheek, and I unwrapped my arms from him and looked up at his face.

"I'm sorry!" We both said it simultaneously, and then laughed.

"I'm sorry I lied about the play."

"*I'm* sorry I said you were ashamed of me."

"I'm not. You know that, right?"

He nodded. "Yeah. I just know all of those rich Baxter guys have got to be crazy in love with you, and I'm lucky if I have twenty bucks to buy you pizza when the weekend comes."

I reached out and squeezed his hands. "That doesn't matter to me."

"Listen, Lulu . . . I have something really important to tell you. To show you, actually."

"What?"

He pulled his cell phone from his back pocket. "I heard about how it went down. I actually know one of the guys you played against. I've beaten him pretty badly myself. Terrible player. The guy with the cheesy mustache."

I squinted as I tried to remember him. "Oh, yeah. He was at one of the other tables."

"Yeah, well, I did some asking around. And then I tracked down the Pokerfiend. Al Martinelli. And look."

He had opened his phone—it was the kind that could take a picture. I looked at the photo he'd snapped. I grabbed it and pulled it closer to my face. "Is that who I think it is?"

Mark nodded.

I threw my arms around his neck again and kissed him on the lips. "You are my most favorite person in the whole world right about now. Come on. You have to show this to my parents and the mayor."

Mark shook his head. "They'll never approve of me, Lulu."

I looked up at him and took his hand. "Mark, they're just going to have to see past the earring and the tattoo to the nice guy underneath."

"I took the picture for *you*, Lulu. You just take it up to them."

"No. When they see this, they're going to know how much you care about me."

I saw him struggling to decide, so I just started walking toward my dad's building, sort of pulling him along. "Come on."

We climbed up the staircase and walked into the apartment together, which was still overcrowded with bodyguards, the mayor, and my parents. Mom eyed Mark up and down. No, he was no Baxter boy. He had on jeans, a sweatshirt, and an earring. He unzipped his sweatshirt and took it off, revealing a Harley T-shirt—and his tattoo. He stuck his hand out to Mom and then the mayor. I could tell it was a firm handshake—an important move, since my mom calls anyone who doesn't shake firmly a "limp fish."

"Mark O'Malley." He nodded at the bodyguards. I half expected them to frisk him.

"Um . . ." He stammered for a moment. "I have something important to tell you all."

"Yes?" David asked.

Mark looked around at the small crowd filling Dad's tiny living room to capacity.

"Well . . . when I heard what happened, I started asking around about the game."

The mayor cocked an eyebrow at Mark.

"Oh, you see, sir . . . I . . . um . . . sometimes play a little backroom poker. And Lulu and I are kind of seeing each other. We *are* seeing each other." His eyes darted from my mom to my dad. I smiled.

"Anyway," he continued, "you know, being as I play some poker myself, I hear rumors about games. Games like the one Lulu played. They're held regularly by a group that call themselves the Turks, for the young turks of Wall Street. You know—hotshots. But that guy Al Martinelli? The one who was behind the film the reporters keep mentioning?"

"Yeah." I leaned forward. "He calls himself Pokerfiend on e-mail."

"Well, get a load of this. Guess who he works for? Unofficially."

"Who?" David asked.

"Yeah, who?" my dad chimed in.

"Lawton Horne."

"Oh, my gracious," my mom said, her hand flying to her mouth.

The mayor asked, "How can you be sure?"

"It was word on the street. So I followed him. And . . ." He took out his cell phone. "I snapped this picture this morning."

Lawton Horne was the mayor's chief rival if and when he declared his candidacy for reelection. And Lawton Horne was huddling with Al Martinelli over coffee in the picture.

"Could the whole thing—I mean, every last bit of it—be a setup by Horne? Forget the whole investor story," I said.

"I don't know. Politics is a dirty business," the mayor mused. "But involving my own stepdaughter . . . that's a new low, even for Horne."

"Mark." My dad clapped him on the shoulder. "We owe you one."

"I just want to be able to see Lulu."

Suddenly I wished it were Mark and me, alone, without bodyguards, without anyone around. Just so I could kiss him again.

He was, I was sure, my king of hearts.

Chapter Nineteen

Lulu's Rule of Poker #19:
Know who you can count on when the chips are down.

I was dressed like the perfect conservative Tallulah Elizabeth King of Baxter Academy. My mom had bought me a Chanel suit that made me feel like I was fifty years old. It was black with white trim and gold buttons. I wore sensible black pumps and panty hose. My hair was blown straight and gleamed with products, and they had hired a makeup artist to work her wonders on my face so that I looked like an all-American girl instead of an all-American juvenile delinquent with a retainer and a Hello Kitty shirt, like the evening news showed.

The mayor was at a podium in front of the fire-place at Gracie Mansion. My mother was to his right. His campaign people were to his left. And me? I was right next to him—between him and Mom—and he was holding my hand.

"Ladies and gentlemen of the press . . . ," he began, leaning forward ever so slightly into the bank of microphones. There had to have been forty of them. The national news had picked up the story—lucky me. "I know you've been waiting a couple of days for a statement, but I believe in being honest. I believe in having all the facts. I wanted to wait until I was sure of what I was going to say, sure of the facts. So here I am."

Click-click-click went dozens and dozens of cameras. The flashes made me see spots. I looked out in the seats and I spied Mark and Dad and Grandpa and Grandfather. Mark winked at me. Grandfather gave me a thumbs-up sign.

"Of course, by now everyone knows that my beloved future stepdaughter, Tallulah King, was involved in a gambling incident. That is unfortunate. Tallulah is an excellent cardplayer." He looked over at me and smiled. "And I suppose that's not a typical hobby for young ladies, but she can hold her own at the poker table, or so I am told."

He paused. Man, he was good. The press was eating out of his hand. It wasn't so much what he was saying—though that was part of it. He was just so polished and smooth, like he was telling a simple story.

"Between friends, where Tallulah usually plays, poker can be a fun pastime. I know poker playing amongst young people has risen. Poker is on national television. It's become an 'in' sport. But unfortunately, some very nefarious and manipulative people tried to blackmail Tallulah into playing high-stakes—and highly illegal—poker. She knows this is wrong and accepts the consequences of those actions. But at its root, she was first trying to help a friend."

I looked out at the audience and saw Dack and his mother. And to my shock, there was Dack's dad. And Baywatch. And Baywatch's outfit was remarkably modest. Usually her tops are cut so low you can practically see her nipples.

"Then," the mayor went on, "she was filmed and a blackmail arrangement was proposed. The individual who allegedly blackmailed her—and we have her laptop as confirmation of all this—is now in custody. And as you all know by now, through various leaks in the press, that person is a close associate of Lawton

Horne, who recently announced a run for the office of mayor of New York City."

I saw reporters scribbling furiously.

"I am convinced, when this is all completely unraveled, that Tallulah will quite clearly be seen as a victim in all this. And that some villains in the top echelons of dirty New York politics will have to face the consequences of their actions."

The mayor paused. "I have something else to say. This isn't on my scripted statement. It's not on a teleprompter. This is from my heart. I want to say that I admire Tallulah very much. And I care about her very much. You know, it's too easy to try to sum up a person with sound bites. The complexity of it all is that Tallulah was trying very hard to help a friend who was in a jam. And then, amazingly, she was trying to avoid embarrassing her new soon-to-be stepfather. She was trying not to upset her mother. She was trying to do the right thing, on her own."

My mother dabbed at her eyes with a tissue she was clutching. She was in a Dior suit in muted pink and looked like a darn *Town & Country* cover model.

"It takes courage to try to do the right thing. Tallulah didn't know what she was walking into when she entered that game with people twice her age. She knew only that she didn't want a tape of her making its way to all of you." He smiled at the press corps. "You know, you all can be pretty tough when you're onto a hot story."

The press laughed, and the room's mood lightened.

"Finally, Tallulah didn't ask to be in a fishbowl. She didn't ask for you all to be following her every move as the mayor's stepdaughter. I am, indeed, going to run again. And I hope to win the election, with my new wife and stepdaughter by my side. But I hope you will allow Tallulah to be who she is. She likes poker. She likes her life with her father. She is a blend of New York. Uptown and downtown. Maybe, in her own way, she is as New York as the Empire State Building. As all of us. And I hope you will allow her to be precisely who she is. Thank you."

There was silence. And then, amazingly, the press corps burst into applause. I smiled. I love New York.

Chapter Twenty

Lulu's Rule of Poker #20:
A royal straight flush is the best there is.

My mother opted to wear ivory, not white. She chose a Vera Wang gown in silk that slid over her body and made her look like a Greek goddess.

I was thankful she did not choose pink for her bridesmaids' dresses. In fact, I was her lone bridesmaid, and we chose something in elegant silvery blue. As she promised, I was involved with every decision about the wedding, until I wanted to scream. Napkins, china, place settings, centerpieces, the band—no detail was overlooked.

After the mayor's press conference, the papers and television stations had a field day. A few still wanted to make me look like a terrible stepdaughter, but the people of New York—as polled by the *Daily News*—seemed a forgiving lot. Yeah, a few judgmental people thought I should go to court and have a judge throw the book at me. But the overwhelming majority seemed to understand it was about friendship.

My mother and father warmed up to Mark. They were impressed that he was so devoted to me that he got to the bottom of the whole thing. The mayor was impressed enough to give Mark a legitimate job. I mean, it's as a messenger for his office, but now Mark has decided that after high school he will go to community college at night, and then . . . who knows? Maybe he'll get that degree in accounting he talked about. It doesn't matter. What matters is that my family likes him, and someone is giving him a chance to pursue something besides poker. I mean, cards are okay, but it's nice to have a backup plan.

Dack? Well, the entire incident made his father realize that perhaps Baywatch's breasts had blinded him to the fact that his son needed a little guidance and influence. His mother met somebody, too—the head of the mayor's security detail. Now that she had a boyfriend, she wasn't nearly so hysterical, so Dack lucked out.

All in all, the worst poker game of my life turned out to be pretty lucky after all.

When it was time to dance at the "wedding of the year," according to the papers, my father took the first dance with me.

"Maybe now that you're the princess of Gracie Mansion, you shouldn't play poker anymore, Lulu," he said as he twirled me around to a slow song.

"Didn't you hear the mayor, Dad? I'm a blend of both worlds. I'm not going to change. Come on . . . what about Grandpa's dream of backing me in the World Series of Poker?"

"That would be something, wouldn't it?"

I nodded. "Dad . . . just because I'm a part of this world doesn't mean that I don't adore your world too."

Just then the mayor cut in. Dad kissed my cheek, and David twirled me away to the center of the dance floor as the band played "The Way You Look Tonight."

"And how's the most beloved girl in New York City?" he asked me.

"That's just until the next mess I get into."

"Every woman with an eligible son is aiming for you, Lulu."

"I'll stick with Mark."

"Thanks, you know."

"For what?"

"Well, this whole thing started with you not wanting that file clip to go to the media. You could have not cared."

"You make my mother happy."

"Are you sorry you have to come live here?"

I shrugged. "As long as you don't mind Angie and Dack, and Mark . . . and the occasional poker game . . . and us eating you out of house and home."

"I kind of like the commotion."

"You know you're going to win by a landslide."

Lawton Horne, no matter how many weak denials he issued, couldn't recover from the revelation that Pokerfiend was on his payroll.

The mayor nodded. "I know. Then who knows? Maybe I'll run for president."

"Poker in the White House."

"Frankly, if that's the biggest scandal of my presidency, we're doing okay, Lulu."

The two of us laughed. Then Mark came over

and cut in. The mayor kissed my cheek and stepped away, and Mark took me in his arms.

"You look beautiful, Lulu."

"Thanks. You look pretty darn handsome yourself." Mark was wearing a tux.

"You sure you don't want to trade me in for one of the Baxter Academy boys?"

"Why settle for a measly three of a kind when you can have a royal straight flush?"

"That's my girl." He kissed me.

It was then that I decided poker was a lot like love: When you're dealt a good hand, you should bet all your chips and go for broke.

Lulu's Poker Games

Dear Readers:

Poker is a game. It can be fun to win a few dollars playing with friends, but never bet what you can't afford to lose.

Also, some people just shouldn't gamble at all, period. They feel an addictive tendency when they play. This is called "chasing your losses." If you lose at poker and feel like you can't stop playing until you win back all your money, you may have a problem controlling your betting. If you think that might be you or a friend, contact Gamblers Anonymous.

Okay . . . now I've compiled some games to try. Remember my rules. And have fun!

Lulu

Glossary of Common Poker Slang

(so you can sound like you know what you're talking about)

ALL IN: My favorite things to do, this is when you bet it all—all your chips—you're "all in." When you watch poker, this is when the big gamblers push their pile of chips into the middle of the table. Gotta love betting big! (Okay, so when I play with friends, this might mean a whopping four dollars. Still . . . it's fun to act like a big shot.)

ANTE: This is the set amount each player must put into the middle before the start of a hand of poker. It might be money (like a nickel), or a chip, or . . .

if playing strip poker with Dack, it might mean a sock.

BET: Placing a wager into the pot on any round. Might be a nickel, a chip, or Dack's sock. See also ANTE.

BUTTON: When you play Texas Hold 'Em, someone is the designated dealer—and they have the "button" spot.

CARDS SPEAK: The face value of your hand regardless of what you say you have. Huh? Put it this way: Sometimes when you play poker, you play with people who don't totally know what they are doing, especially when you're playing for fun. So someone may say they have a straight to the nine, but then they put down their cards and they actually have a straight flush to the nine. Well, they win over someone with just a straight, even if they didn't "announce" or say it right.

CHECK: When you opt not to bet or raise right off the bat. You wait until one of your opponents bets or raises. This can be a strategy. Or you might be running out of money!

COMMON CARD: A card dealt faceup (so you can see it, versus down) when there's a "showdown" in stud poker. Sometimes there aren't enough cards left in the deck at the very end (like if everyone trades in three or four cards, depending on how many are sitting at the table), so you use a common card.

COMMUNITY CARDS: These cards are dealt faceup (versus not being able to see them) in the center of the table and can be used by all players to make their best hand when you play Hold 'Em and some other games.

CUT: To "cut" the deck into two sections after the dealer shuffles.

CUT CARD: The bottom card.

DEAD MAN'S HAND: A pair of aces and a pair of eights. Supposedly Wyatt Earp was shot while holding the dead man's hand, and it's considered a bad-luck hand in poker. Yup, poker players are superstitious.

DEAL: To give each player cards, or put cards on the table. "Deal me in!"

DECK: A set of playing cards. There are fifty-two cards in a standard deck. If you play with the joker for a wild card, then you have fifty-three. Yeah, I'm good with math.

DEUCE: A two card (the number two).

DISCARD: In a draw game, you throw card(s) out of your hand to make room for new (and hopefully better) cards, or the card(s) thrown away; some players call it your muck. I could think of a few other choice words, but I promised my mother I wouldn't curse.

DOWN CARDS: Cards that are dealt facedown.

DRAW: This is when you play a draw poker game. You replace the cards you don't like for new—and hopefully better—ones.

FACE CARD: A king, queen, or jack.

FIXED LIMIT: Presetting the limit on bets. For example, a common betting structure among friends would be "nickel ante," where you put a nickel in for the beginning ante, or "pot," and then you can start betting in dime increments or higher once someone has a pair or better showing (in seven-card stud).

FLOP: In Texas Hold 'Em or Omaha, the three community cards that are turned after the first round of betting. They get turned over, one after the other.

FLUSH: A poker hand with five cards of the same suit. A good hand! (A flush beats a straight. Remember that!)

FOLD: Well, you got a bad hand, so you quit that round and *fold* your cards until the next hand.

FORCED BET: When you play stud, you often force people to bet (let's say a nickel) just to stay in the first round.

FOURTH STREET: The second faceup card in seven-card stud or the first board card after the flop in Texas Hold 'Em (also called the turn card). It sounds kind of cool. "We're rounding Fourth Street!"

FULL HOUSE: A hand consisting of three of a kind and a pair. Some people say "full boat." When you show your cards, you'd say something like, "Full boat, pretty ladies over eights." (Translation? Queens and eights.)

HAND: The cards you have in your hand when you're playing. (By that, I mean what's on the table for you to use, plus physically what is *in* your hand.)

HOLE CARDS: The cards dealt facedown to a player. Shhh . . . you don't show anyone your hole cards.

INSURANCE: A side agreement when someone is all in. A player puts up money that guarantees a payoff of a set amount in case the other guy wins the pot. Just like an insurance policy.

JOKER: The joker can be a wild card, and in games of high and low, you sometimes use the joker. That's the card with the funny-looking guy on it.

KANSAS CITY LOWBALL: A form of draw poker. Get this . . . the best hand is 7-5-4-3-2, and straights and flushes count *against* you, not for you. Yeah. Confusing.

LOWBALL: A draw game where the lowest hand wins. Good for people with bad luck!

MISDEAL: A mistake when you're dealing so that you have to deal again. For example, you are supposed to deal someone a card facedown, but accidentally you show the card. Oops. Misdeal! (It's the poker version of a do-over.)

MUCK: The pile of discards, or cards you don't want. The dealer collects them—and it's important that they stay *facedown*.

NO LIMIT: A betting structure where you can bet any or all of your chips in one bet. But remember . . . if you bet it *all*, you can lose it *all*!

OPENER: The player who makes the first bet.

RAISE: To increase the amount of a previous bet. This increase may have to meet certain table or house rules. If it's at my house, they're my rules. At Dack's house, he can decide. For instance, among friends, you often play that you can raise an unlimited amount only on the very last card, and prior to that you can raise only in nickel or dime increments.

RERAISE: To raise someone else's raise. (You know, like in the movies, where someone says, "I'll see your raise and raise you one better!")

SIDE POT: A separate pot. Sometimes when I play seven-card stud, I play a side pot of a quarter for each player for the highest heart card. Then the person with the highest heart (ace, king, on down to whoever has the highest heart) who also stays in to the end, wins the side pot.

SHUFFLE: When the dealer mixes the cards before a hand.

SPLIT POT: A pot that is divided among players, because of either a tie for the best hand or sometimes an agreement. This is often a way to build up a bigger pot, because someone is more likely to stay in if they think they have one of two shots at winning—or splitting—the pot.

STACK: Chips in front of a player. I like nice, tall stacks of chips.

STRAIGHT: Five cards in consecutive order.

STRAIGHT FLUSH: Five cards in consecutive order and also the same suit. Trust me . . . this is a good hand!

STREET: Cards that are dealt on a particular round in stud games. For instance, the fourth card in a player's hand is often known as fourth street, the sixth card as sixth street, and so on. Cool lingo!

TURN CARD: The fourth street card in Texas Hold 'Em or Omaha.

UP CARDS: Cards that are dealt faceup for all players to see in stud games.

WAGER: To bet.

Texas Hold 'Em

It's played like this:

1. The dealer shuffles a standard fifty-two-card deck. He or she should shuffle 'em good. Watch him.

2. Most Texas Hold 'Em poker games start with the two players to the left of the dealer (who is sometimes also called the button) putting a predetermined amount of money into the pot before any cards are dealt. That makes sure there's always money being played for. This is called "posting

the blinds." It's a little complicated, but in plain English, it means there's money in the pot. Yay! It's not fun unless you can win a little something, right? Even if you play for candy! (That's how my dad taught me years ago. We played for Life Savers!)

3. Each player is dealt two cards, facedown. These are known as the "hole cards." Don't show anyone your hole cards.

4. Now the fun part starts. The betting begins. Players can call, raise, or fold when it's their turn to bet.

5. Now for the flop. After the first betting round, the dealer discards the top card of the deck. This is called "burning the card." It helps stop cheats by making sure no one could possibly see the top card, even by accident. But if you're playing with friends, come on . . . no one should be cheating, right? Well, I say that, but my uncle Bernie always cheats. The dealer then flips the next three cards faceup on the table. These cards are called the flop. Now, eventually, five community cards (look in the glossary . . . these are cards anyone can use)

will be placed faceup on the table. Remember, anyone can use them to make their best hand. Players can use any combination of the community cards and their own two hole cards to form the best possible five-card poker hand. Best hand wins.

6. After the flop, another round of betting takes place, beginning with the player to the left of the dealer (who, remember, can be called the button). During this and all the rest of the betting, players can check (remember, that means you don't raise at all but check—do nothing—and see what the next player is going to do), call, raise, or fold when it's their turn to bet.

7. Time to visit Fourth Street. The dealer burns another card (sticks it down to the bottom) and places one more faceup on the table. This fourth community card is called the turn or Fourth Street. The button begins the third round of betting.

8. After Fourth Street comes . . . what else? Fifth Street. The dealer burns another card before placing the final faceup card on the

table. This card is called the "river" or Fifth Street.

9. Now you have to figure out what your hand is going to be. You should be thinking hard now. This is for all the marbles, as they say. Players can now use any combination of seven cards—the five community cards in the middle and the two hole cards (that only *you* know)—to form the best possible five-card poker hand.

10. The fourth and final round of betting starts with the the button. After the final betting round, everyone who is still in the game (who didn't fold) reveals their hands. The player who made the initial bet (if you can think back that far!) or the player who made the last raise shows his or her hand first.

11. Drumroll please! The player with the best hand—five cards—wins!

Okay, so it's a little confusing. But not for me.

Baseball Stud Poker

Several different poker games are played only in low-stakes home poker games (among friends!). Some of these games are called baseball, and generally baseball games mean a lot of wild cards (usually threes and nines, but sometimes other cards), paying a specified amount for wild cards, being able to "buy" another card if you are dealt a four, and many other rules (for example, the queen of spades can be called a "rainout" and ends the hand). These rules are usually pretty silly and fun and vary from house to house and even from one area of the country to the next. For instance, I play that threes and nines are wild, if you get a four you can "buy" another card (usually for a nickel), and if you get dealt a queen of spades, you're out. These same rules can be applied to a "no-peek" poker game, in which case the game is called night baseball. A no-peek game means you get all your cards dealt facedown and no one is allowed to look even at their own cards. Everyone has to stay in until the very end (which is why the pots are bigger) or until they lose to a hand already showing.

So, if you sit to the left of the dealer, you turn over your first card. Let's say it's a measly two. You stop turning cards. You bet—why? Because no one else's cards are showing and therefore you have the "highest" card showing. The next person then starts turning over his or her cards. They stop when they beat your measly two. They bet. Then the next person and so on, and it goes 'round and 'round until the end and the highest hand at the table.

Chicago Stud Poker

The game of Chicago stud poker is a seven-card-stud poker game in which the high poker hand splits the pot with the player who has the highest spade in the *hole* (that's the facedown cards). This is like (look in the glossary) a side pot.

Standard Five-card-draw Poker

Draw poker is very popular in home poker games, but you don't see it in casinos or tournaments very much, because, frankly, it can be boring compared with Hold 'Em or some other types of poker. If you are playing with good players, it can get ho-hum.

To start, each player gets five cards, one at a time, all facedown. (Don't forget to ante first!) The remaining deck is placed to the side while the dealer looks at his or her own hand. All the players, in fact, pick up the cards and hold them in their hands, being careful not to let anyone else see what they have. (Among friends, if you accidentally see someone else's hand, you should do the right thing and 'fess up and redeal the hand.) The first betting round occurs and starts with the player to the dealer's left. If more than one player remains after this round, then you start the "draw" round.

Each player tells the dealer how many cards he or she wants to get rid of, and discards that many from his or her poker hand. Now the dealer picks the deck back up, burns a card (see glossary), and each player gets new cards to replace the exact number they just got rid of. So now everyone has five cards again. A second betting round occurs after the draw phase. If more than one player is left, then you have a showdown, which sounds pretty Wild West, huh?

Now, just like in most poker games played at home and not in a casino, there are house and table rules. In some games I play in, the rule is that a player may not replace more than three cards, unless he or she draws four cards while keeping an ace (or wild card)—and that person flashes that card to the dealer to prove he or she is entitled to four new ones.

Pass-the-trash Draw Poker

This game is also called anaconda poker. Seven cards are dealt to each poker player facedown. Before the first betting round, each player looks at his cards and removes exactly three cards from his hand and places them on the table to his left. In other words, you each get rid of your "trash." After each person has done this, you pick up the cards your right-hand neighbor gave you and place them in your poker hand. You usually then curse at your neighbor because, chances are, they gave you really bad cards! It is important that everyone discard before looking at the cards that he or she is about to get.

After the first passing of trash, you bet. Then you pass your trash again, but this time only two cards. At this point I am usually screaming at Dack. Now you bet. Then you pass the trash again. But this time only *one* card. (Which really stinks if by now you have a good hand and don't really *want* to give away a card!) Finally you bet again, and then it's time to see which player has the best set of five cards.

Follow the Queen

Played like regular seven-card-stud poker, only the card following a queen dealt faceup is wild, and if the last card dealt up is a queen, nothing is wild.

The wild card thus changes—sometimes four times in one game! So, let's say at round one of betting the wild card is a four. The next up card is dealt and someone gets a queen. The very next up card dealt is then a nine. Well, now the fours are no longer wild (too bad for the person with two four cards who was betting big!), and nines are. This is again one of those silly home games.

Hope you've had fun!

About the Author

Liza Conrad is the author of *Rock My World* and *High School Bites*. When she isn't writing, she surrounds herself with pets and friends and family. She really enjoys playing poker and hanging out at her favorite sushi restaurant. She is at work on her next book and can be reached at www.lizaconrad.com.